One Grand Season

by

Sarita Leone

*A Willowbrook Manor Romance,
Book Two*

One Grand Season

COPYRIGHT © 2015 by Sarita Leone

Cover Art by *Debbie Taylor*

The Wild Rose Press, Inc.
PO Box 708
Adams Basin, NY 14410-0708
Visit us at www.thewildrosepress.com

Publishing History
First Tea Rose Edition, 2015
Print ISBN 978-1-62830-803-7
Digital ISBN 978-1-62830-804-4

A Willowbrook Manor Romance, Book Two
Published in the United States of America

"I can only imagine that being married to the wrong woman—say a woman with whom one is not entirely compatible but who does, on the face of things, seem suitable for the position—must be like being led to slaughter. I cannot fathom how hopeless one must feel waking morning after morning beside someone who might be nice but does not stir the heart. It must be…"

Heaving a deep sigh, Will finished, "Like dying. Yes, now that you put it that way I quite agree."

Relief washed over Oliver, brightening his mood. Since last year's chaos he was not fully certain all his views were socially acceptable. There had been too many wild, crazed moments for him to believe he always saw a situation in its proper light.

Will was his voice of reason, and hearing the other's validation sent doubts scurrying.

It was not that Oliver was opposed to marriage. He was not—especially after witnessing his parents' devoted union. But when he married a woman he wanted to be certain he was doing so for the right reason, and not because someone decided it was in his—or her—best interest.

Then he recalled Miss Fox. She wasn't his type, but she had certainly made a lasting impression.

Dedication

Love never dies.

Chapter 1

London, June 1815

Vivian Fox detested being the family's poorest relation.

Fortunately, her mother's second cousin was a woman of heart as well as means, and had generously invited her to spend the summer at Willowbrook Manor. The forty-acre estate lay within London proper, but was far enough removed from the center of Town that the Gregory family and their guests could feel themselves out in the country if they so desired. Had Lady Gregory not been so kind, Vivian would have undoubtedly had another dull Season without any prospect of fun, fancy or—most importantly—spending time with any eligible men.

She had never been to to the country before—she had never been anywhere, really. Her life to this point had centered around the small flat in Stropshire where she and her younger brother lived with their mother. When not busy cleaning the flat or caring for young Liam, she brought extra funds to their meager situation by doing hand sewing for a local seamstress who catered to a wealthy London clientele. Vivian had worked on enough dazzling gowns, elegant morning dresses and pricey afternoon ensembles to identify this year's designs from last. Alas, she herself had never worn, let alone owned, anything as fancy as the items she labored over.

But that was neither here nor there, as far as Vivian was concerned. Life had been filled with harsh realities, and she was fully aware of the difference between the "haves" and the "have-nots." She was under no illusion as to which set the Stropshire Foxes belonged. Accordingly, her realistic nature did not allow for wanting what she could not have.

When the carriage rolled to a stop outside the front entrance of the manor, she was so tired, dusty and travel-worn that her fondest hope for the imminent future included plenty of hot water, soap and the chance to rest.

If she was especially lucky, food might be included, although it was optional. Years of not having enough to eat, or of giving the biggest portion of any morsel to Liam, had left her almost indifferent to food. Again, it was a case of learning not to desire what could not be had. So if sustenance was provided she would gladly eat. If it was not, she would be just as happy with a bowlful of water with which to bathe.

The driver appeared by the side of the carriage. He opened the door, unfolded the metal steps and stood back. He did not offer a hand to help her down, but she did not expect he would. No man had done so on any of the few occasions when she had ridden instead of walked so she clutched the carriage's inside hand strap, forced her cramped leg muscles to support her weight and proceeded to step from the musty confines of the vehicle.

The manor's wide mahogany front door had not yet opened so she stretched, then put a hand behind her and attempted to massage the kink out of her lower back. Cobblestones and ruts did not provide a comfortable journey, especially when trundled over on ancient wooden wheels. It was a miracle the decrepit vehicle had not broken down along the way. But her passage had been within her budget so when faced with the prospect of riding in a newer, pricier coach or this one, she had naturally chosen economy over comfort.

Vivian took a deep breath, thankful to finally not inhale stale air or the dust thrown up by the horses' hooves. She looked toward the front of the building. Not even her wildest imaginings prepared her for what she saw.

The manor was built of smooth gray stone, much of it moss-covered or draped with runners of deep green ivy. Two turrets jutted toward the sky, making the structure seem more castle-like than manor-ish. It was enormous but not ostentatious. It looked like it had grown naturally from the earth beneath it, retaining the rustic feel of a country home while giving the appearance of welcome.

She loved it immediately. The front flower beds were a riot of color, the grassy area just beyond the stone drive looked verdant enough to make her want to kick off her side-button shoes and run barefoot . At the far northern edge of the building, a fountain burbled.

It is like a fairytale.

The front door opened wide, a gray-haired butler in full uniform holding the door latch in a hand encased in a snowy white glove. His appearance reminded Vivian of her own griminess. Had there been a way to hide until she had a chance to freshen up she would have done so. Unfortunately, that was still one more option not open to her so she squared her shoulders, stiffened her spine and took a step forward. She only got two paces closer to the door before she stumbled, the pins-and-needles sensation in her toes hindering her movement. Limbs trembled, and for a panic-filled instant she was certain she was going to fall face-first onto the stones at her feet.

The driver had left the side of the carriage, so he no longer stood directly behind her. His job was nearly finished. He had delivered her and as soon as he got her small trunk down from the luggage rack he was free to leave, having earned every shilling of his fare. Occupied as he was, had he been inclined to reach out to steady her (which she sincerely doubted, his having shown no interest whatsoever in her well-being at any point in the journey) she was completely beyond the length of his arms.

"Miss!"

The butler saw her plight but he was too far to be of any service. He would never reach her before she fell, and although he scrambled forward Vivian knew she could not depend on him for help. It seemed her fate in life that she take care of herself, without relying on anyone else's assistance.

In one very unladylike *whoosh!* all air left her lungs as she bent forward from the waist.

I am going down, she thought with sudden clarity. There is no help for it, I am fall—

Just when there seemed no way out of her chin meeting the ground, she was lifted to her feet by an unseen force. A solid, warm wall of navy blue surrounded her and held her upright as her blood thundered in her head. Struggling to catch her breath, she gasped, deeply inhaling a spicy scent. It sent her senses reeling and her knees began to buckle.

Realization hit her hard. A man! Now that her wits were returning, she noticed the blue cocoon which held her so securely had muscles. There was movement beneath the fabric pressed against her nose. Then there was space before her and she found herself gazing up into the face of a very good-looking man. His mouth formed a perfect "o" and his coffee-colored eyes were circles of alarm.

"I say, are you all right? Do you need to be carried?" The gentleman's words smacked of culture and education. His way of life no doubt included rescuing damsels in distress on a habitual basis, but she was not any damsel and had no intention of acting as if she needed rescuing. Immediately she began to pull herself from his grasp, but his grip was firm and he did not let go. She could have fought more strenuously but she already felt silly enough.

I have made a cake of myself, and I am not even past the front door!

The butler stood beside the young man who stubbornly kept his hands on her shoulders. The older man's face was white with concern, and she regretted having frightened him.

Waving a hand in front of her face, she attempted to diminish the situation.

"I am fine, really." The sooner she extricated herself from the notice of these men—both figuratively and literally—the better. "I am just—" Her gaze darted past the butler to yet another man who ran down the steps to join the cluster. The deep blue eyes, as dark and mysterious as she imagined the ocean must be, stared into her face. When their gazes met, and held, all rational thought flew from her mind, merely wisps of intelligence torn to flimsy threads by a passing breeze. Her tongue felt glued to the roof of her mouth, and she would have stood and stared—endlessly, perhaps—had the man who held her not given her a gentle shake.

He caught her attention, and she turned back to him.

"Are you certain you are really fine?" His question was insistent, no longer reactionary but genuinely concerned.

Wearily, Vivian nodded. The bonnet ribbons tied beneath her chin had long since given up any appearance of being starched, and dragged like two sodden kite tails against her neck. She knew she must look awful. Coupled with her graceless behavior, she would not be surprised if these people ordered the coachman to put her trunk back in its place on the rack and insisted she depart this very minute. Had she been in their place she might have done just that, so she bore them no ill will if that was their plan.

They still stared, so she answered, "I am fine. Really and truly fine. I am just..." The effort of speaking was too much. Assembling coherent thoughts, and then getting them from her mind to their ears, was too great a task so she closed her mouth with a snap and heaved a sigh.

"You are tired." The man beside the butler swept a glance down to her feet, then back up to her face. "Do you think you have your legs back yet? Can you walk?"

She nodded, grateful for his insight. "I am fine now."

Remembering her manners, Vivian gasped and

tried to dip into a curtsey. It was painful, but her toes, calves and thighs were no longer numb. Her mother had gone over the first meeting so many times, and had made her promise she would not disgrace her by failing to bob during her introduction, that there was no alternative other than to bend her knees and incline her head.

The man who held her would not allow her to lower herself more than a scant half-inch before he realized her intent and pulled her upward. "I am glad you are restored." Then, as if he had not just cut short her first curtsey at the Manor, he smiled and said, "You must be Miss Fox. My mother has been anxiously waiting your arrival. You see, since my sister Lucie got married there is no female in residence for her to chatter with. She is overjoyed you consented to visit with us. We all are."

As he spoke, he released her. By the time he finished, she stood on her own.

"That is kind of you to say." He made it sound as if she had done them a favor by visiting, when it was so clearly the other way around. The magnanimous statement left her at a loss, but that did not matter.

Now that she was not falling at his feet, the gentleman seemed much more at ease, smiling and placing his now-free hand over the center of his starched white shirt.

"I apologize. I have not introduced myself, have I? I am Oliver Gregory. Welcome to Willowbrook Manor. Hastings, will you see to Miss Fox's trunk, please?"

The butler gave a small bow. "Certainly, sir." Turning to the driver, he motioned toward the door and the two men proceeded to the front entrance. The servant reached into his vest pocket, pulled out a coin and handed it to the other man after her trunk had been deposited just inside the door.

"Miss Fox, may I escort you inside?" Oliver Gregory held out an arm so she tucked hers beneath his. He felt solid and strong, and she leaned on him as they slowly walked to the gaping front door.

The spectacle she created upon her arrival was nothing like what she had envisioned in her mind— what she had hoped for, actually—but for better or worse, at least she had arrived. There had to be something said for finding the end of one's journey, even if the finding was only temporary.

Vivian decided as she stepped from her old world into the new that she was going to enjoy every exciting moment of this summer. After all, it would most likely be the only opportunity she would ever have to experience one grand Season.

****

Oliver Hazelton Gregory was used to getting his own way.

His life had been one of ease which was fitting since he was the only son of a well-off duke. Never had he known hardship or want, at least not with regard to the fundamental issues in life—food, clothing, shelter. Even all entertainment and educational opportunities afforded him were of a high standard, and he had availed himself of each prospect his family's fortune provided. Yes, the next duke of Danbury had eagerly walked through every single door opened to him by his very presence in the Gregory family.

The future duke did not have a completely skeleton-free closet, however. Oliver had fought demons, struggled against a dependence on medicinal products and battled his conscience for having been weak enough to succumb to that which could only do him serious harm—if not be the cause of his premature death. It had been a horrifying descent into near-madness and an agonizing crawl back to sanity, but he had overcome the terrors his addiction wrought.

One year had come and gone, and Oliver was still healthy. The family doctor assured him he was cured, but he could not fully believe that. It was a luxury, a fable invented to soothe, he was sure. And as much as Oliver wished—nee, craved—to be relieved of the mental burden he carried, he could not blithely believe everything the good doctor said.

He had fallen once. What was to stop him from doing so a second time? Fear that he might give in to temptation could be tamed by day but his sleeping hours were filled with nightmares that left him drenched in sweat and clutching the bedclothes as if all the demons of the underworld stood at the foot of his bed.

Being born into a world of privilege did not guarantee an unblemished existence.

In an effort to keep his days so filled with acceptable endeavors, he had, since his recovery, thrown himself full-tilt into pastimes which were favorably looked upon by those in his social circle. Horseback riding, hunting, polishing his whist skills until he was sought out at parties, dancing, attending musicales, reading and going to the theatre all gave him ample opportunity to prove to himself that he would someday be able to take his place in the long and distinguished line of Gregory men without shame.

His latest undertaking was the planning of a fox hunt. While he found no joy in riding about after small, long-tailed brown animals, he knew others in his set did. Since the family property was vast by comparison to other London-area residences, it seemed logical to host a sporting event on the premises. His peers had begged him all winter long to pull together a fox hunting party and even though he believed deep in his heart that the sight of full-grown men astride massive horses chasing down prey no larger than an ordinary housecat was nothing short of ridiculous, he could not continue to turn them down. Finally, about mid-March, he had consented to the affair. Now all he had to do was plan, and then execute, the gathering.

It was fortunate, not only for Oliver but for his guests as well, that he had in his employ a man who seemed capable of doing absolutely anything asked of him. William Fulbright had once been his valet, an arrangement that worked magnificently for both of them. However, after the madness surrounding his addiction had been put to rest, Oliver knew that the man who kept his secrets, held him through the agony of withdrawal and then nursed him back to health deserved more than a position as valet. After all, anyone could hold his undershorts open and choose his cravats but there were blessed few who could have done what William had.

Now the position of valet was held by a capable young man named Charlie. He was the young son of one of the downstairs housemen, and had proved himself as competent at coordinating his lordship's outfits as his father did at arranging the dining room furniture for dinner parties. All in all, the situation suited everyone involved.

William held a piece of paper loosely in one hand, a pencil in the other, as he walked beside him. They discussed the details of the upcoming fox hunt while strolling in the garden beside the greenhouse. It was a secluded area, and good for thinking.

Oliver slapped his fist against his right thigh. The smack brought a sting, as he had intended it would. There were still times when he could not concentrate on the task at hand no matter how hard he tried to focus. His mind still seemed addled by the remnants of the substances he had poisoned his body with, and although he fought to reclaim every last bit of his cognitive abilities his brain did not always comply.

Botheration! There are details for the fox hunt to go over, yet I cannot get her eyes out of my head. They are haunting me…

"Did you notice her eyes, Will?"

"Your Grace?"

He scowled. He hated being called that. Someday he would have no choice in the matter but right now the address was like sandpaper rubbed on an open wound. One should deserve a superior acknowledgment. Oliver did not feel worthy of the label.

Will, on the other hand, knew his lot in life required he speak in a certain manner to the man in whose service he was. On the matter of proper address, he would not budge. Oliver knew—they had brooked the argument repeatedly.

A truce of sorts had been reached. It was an accommodation which both could tolerate.

When in the company of others, Will was called William by Oliver. Conversely, when anyone might hear them, the assistant spoke deferentially to his employer. Otherwise, they were simply Will and Oliver, more friends than anything else. Had Will been born to a different family and had the same opportunities open to Oliver, they would have undoubtedly been the best of friends. Even without that circumstance, they were as close as brothers. Last year's trial by fire had brought their relationship to the point, and there was no returning to the servant and master dynamic, at least not where it counted—in their hearts.

"Stop that, right this minute. We are alone, with no one to overhear." He shot an annoyed look to his companion. Will was not cowed by the display of displeasure. He grinned like a cat with a mouse hidden behind his molars. Knowing he would get nothing more than the idiotic smirk, he repeated the question. "Did you see her eyes?"

"Her eyes? Of course I saw them. They were right there in the middle of her face, weren't they?"

With a sigh, Oliver nodded toward a stone bench set beneath a towering oak tree. The tree was at least a hundred years old, with a broad canopy of branches that seemed capable of withstanding any storm. They sat on the bench, and rested their backs against the tree trunk.

"Don't be a clown. It doesn't suit you, my friend."

"Why are you so taken with the young lady's eyes?" Will shoved the pencil and paper into his jacket pocket. They were not going to make lists or discuss details, that much was apparent. "It is not like you to be struck speechless by a woman's eyes. Why, you generally pay more attention to her figure. The visitor, from what I could see, is nearly figureless, she is so thin. Not your type at all, is she?"

The truth smacked Oliver in the face. Will was right. Typically he preferred women with curves, someone who did not look like she needed saving from her own self-denial. Secondly, he sought out women who were well-read and could chat about familiar topics. Theatre productions, current events, recent fiction novels...those were the interests he enjoyed discussing with a woman—regardless of the color of her eyes.

What am I thinking? She is entirely unsuitable...but those eyes...

"I cannot deny what you say." In the flower bed beside the greenhouse, scarlet roses had begun to bloom. A sweet scent, tinged with a hint of spiciness, filled the air. His maternal grandmother had planted the hedge long before his father was born. As a boy Oliver had braved the needle-sharp thorns to pick armfuls for his mother. Now, he admired the blooms from a distance, taking a deep whiff of the cloying scent before continuing. "You are right. Mother's guest is much less..." He glanced over his shoulder to be certain they were alone. "She is considerably less well-endowed than normally attracts me. Even if that weren't the case, she does not seem, at least not if our first meeting is any realistic indication, to be someone who might share my interests."

The woman could not manage to elegantly remove herself from a carriage. She had practically fallen at his feet and, even after she claimed to be "fine" she could barely string enough coherent words together to manage minimal conversation.

No, she was definitely not his type.

This might be a long Season, he thought.

Oliver once again slapped his thigh, this time in a burst of annoyance. Leave it to his mother to dream up a scheme to find him a wife—for that was surely what this summer's visitor was, a potential matrimonial match.

"I will not do it, you know. I adore Mother but I will not be pushed into becoming engaged with some church mouse-poor distant relation she believes will be a steadying influence on me. I flatly refuse to do it!"

Will shrugged a philosophical shoulder. "I do not recall your mother asking you to wed the newcomer. Did she do so when I was not present?"

"Of course not. If she had done such a thing you would have surely been the first to know—if only to keep me from drowning in the brandy bottle." The last was a joke, which they each acknowledged with smiles. He did not imbibe in alcohol at all, having learned a lesson about overindulgence he now applied to anything with even the slightest hint of addictive potential. "No, Mother has not mentioned marriage to me since announcing her cousin's daughter was coming to visit. She is much smarter than that, old man. My mother has more up her sleeve than she lets on, even to Father."

"Of that there can be no doubt." Will chuckled.

The Gregory marriage was somewhat unusual in that both partners shared fairly identical footing, and each kept a different—yet equally effective—store of tactics by which marital harmony was maintained. Lord Gregory had no lack of candor, making his intentions simple to decipher. His wife, on the other hand, was much more subtle in the manner with which she brought about what she thought appropriate for the family.

"If my mother wants Miss Fox to find a husband who will better her circumstances—and there can be nothing else Mother might wish for her—she will pull out all the stops to achieve that goal. I pray I am not the fatted calf ready to be lead to slaughter, although I believe I just might be, at that."

"Are you saying marriage is like being slaughtered?" Will's eyebrows lifted so high they disappeared beneath the fringe of chestnut brown curls on his forehead. "Is that what you're saying?"

"No, no, of course not." Oliver paused, and then shook his head, hoping to find a clear thought amidst the jumble racing through his mind. "At least I don't think that's what I'm saying." He stopped again, stared at the ground between his toes for a long moment, and then said, "No. I am most definitely not saying that marriage is like being slaughtered."

Will let out a short laugh. "Well that's a relief!"

Oliver turned to face him, hoping to find assurance in the other man's eyes. Serious thoughts occupied his mind. They were spurred on by the appearance of their houseguest but they had been ideas he had mulled over for some time. Perhaps now was the appropriate time to give a voice to his views.

"I can only imagine that being married to the wrong woman—say a woman with whom one is not entirely compatible but who does, on the face of things, seem suitable for the position—must be like being led to slaughter. I cannot fathom how hopeless one must feel waking morning after morning beside someone who might be nice but does not stir the heart. It must be…"

Heaving a deep sigh, Will finished, "Like dying. Yes, now that you put it that way I quite agree."

Relief washed over Oliver, brightening his mood. Since last year's chaos he was not fully certain all his views were socially acceptable. There had been too many wild, crazed moments for him to believe he always saw a situation in its proper light.

Will was his voice of reason, and hearing the other's validation sent doubts scurrying.

It was not that Oliver was opposed to marriage. He was not—especially after witnessing his parents' devoted union. But when he married a woman he wanted to be certain he was doing so for the right reason, and not because someone decided it was in his—or her—best interest.

Then he recalled Miss Fox. She wasn't his type, but she had certainly made a lasting impression.

With a burst of enthusiasm, he turned, grabbed the other man's wrist and gave it a squeeze. The effect was instantaneous. Will gave him his undivided attention.

"Her eyes! Did you see her eyes, Will? I mean, did you really see them?"

"Of course I did, although I must admit that it took a while before the truth sank in. I saw, but I did not believe *my* eyes. When I finally reached the steps and she looked at me my heart stopped—only for a moment, mind you, but there is no other way to put it. Actually, it was as if everything stopped, just for a second, when she looked at me." Raking his hand through his hair and sending his curls standing on end, he shook his head in disbelief. "Her eyes…they were…"

"Lavender. I have never seen anyone with lavender eyes before but it was no trick. Her eyes were really and truly nearly purple," Oliver finished.

They sat back against the tree trunk, each once again lost in his own musings. After a few minutes, Will broke the silence.

"Saints preserve us—a woman with lavender eyes at Willowbrook. What on earth will happen next?"

Chapter 2

"I am so happy you have come to stay with us, my dear. I have been begging your mother for years to allow you to visit. She always seems to have other plans for you."

Lady Gregory's sitting room was a riot of pastels, palest pink and butter yellow melding effortlessly and giving the feeling of being inside a fabulous painting. The surroundings were homey, yet obviously expensive, and, most importantly, immeasurably welcoming.

She knew all too well what other plans her mother had for her. Vivian had never been without work to occupy her hands or lessons to fill her mind. She taught Liam while she sewed, so her mother's claim there were plans for her was the plain truth.

Setting her teacup carefully on its matching rose-adorned saucer, and then placing the pair on the low wooden table beside her armchair, Vivian formulated a suitable reply. She was fearful of once again making a fool of herself, so she guarded her words more judiciously than was ordinarily her manner.

Hours had passed since she had created a spectacle in the front drive but she still felt the heat of embarrassment upon her cheeks. The butler had given orders she be shown immediately to her rooms, where a hot bath as well as a pot of tea arrived almost at the same instant as she. Once she had refreshed herself, she was grateful when a maid knocked and said Lady Gregory wondered if she was up to taking tea with her.

Meeting her mother's cousin did not have any of the awkwardness she thought it might. Lady Gregory was a charming, gracious hostess who put her somewhat at ease in no time at all.

Still, she had no intention of letting her guard down too far. She had done so earlier, and look at how *that* had turned out.

"Yes, well my mother does need my help, you know." She spread her hands in the air in front of her, palms raised to the ceiling.

Lady Gregory already knew the truth about her cousin's living conditions, so why pretend about any of it?

The Foxes were poor, and needed every shilling they could get. It would not be long before Liam was old enough to do odd jobs, and while neither Vivian nor her mother would wish the little fellow's childhood shortened they would have no choice but to allow him to earn whatever he could.

"I understand that, my dear." The eyes that held her gaze were compassionate. She was glad there was not pity lurking in their depths because pity for pity's sake seemed a waste of energy. Her newfound relation seemed above such nonsense, thankfully. "I also understand that you are quite an accomplished seamstress. Your mother's letters indicate that you have worked on gowns that are sold in some of the City's most elite shops."

Modesty kept her from doing more than giving Lady Gregory a fast nod. "It is true. I am fortunate to have found a situation that allows me to stay at home with my brother while I work. It is, I think, the best of circumstances for someone like me, to be able to tend to family matters while putting food on the dinner table."

Immediately Vivian regretted her words.

The idea that her hostess might believe her mother had sent her in search of a handout chilled her blood. She put her hand over her chest, where her heart fluttered madly, and shook her head.

"Oh! I did not mean that how it came out—I-I— why, I only meant that there would be no one to watch Liam if I went out to a shop all day. He cannot be left alone in the flat—at least he could not, when he was smaller, you know. But now he is old enough to be left on his own—for short spells, mind—although Mother and I both worry when there is no one to supervise him." She was babbling, but there seemed no way to stem the flood once it had begun. "Boys—they will be boys, you know."

Lady Gregory stared at her for a heartbeat. Then, she threw her head back and laughed. Vivian was momentarily stunned but there seemed nothing else to do so she released the breath she had been holding and smiled. The release, and Lady Gregory's apparent understanding, steadied her nerves. The past days had left them frayed, and with the debacle upon her arrival and now this unfortunate conversation she was nearly done to a tick.

"Oh!" Her hostess, impeccably groomed and wearing a tea dress of the softest-looking fabric imaginable, flapped a hand before her cheeks. Apples bloomed on her creamy complexion, making her look like a schoolgirl wearing adult clothing. The laughter had disturbed her upsweep, and a curl dangled by Lady Gregory's right ear. It hung beside an emerald earring whose color matched exactly the shade of its owner's dress.

"Are you all right? Shall I find someone?" When Vivian rose, thinking to find a cool glass of water for her hostess, she was waved her back into her seat. Slowly, and somewhat reluctantly, she sat.

"Oh, I am fine, really I am," Lady Gregory gasped. A bubble of laughter escaped her lips as she touched a lace-edged hanky to her eyes.

It was Vivian's experience that those who claimed to be fine were the ones who were the furthest from the state. She knew, having sworn to be fine when she most definitely was not.

"Are you sure you wouldn't care for a glass of water?"

"No, no, my dear. I am really fine—in fact, I think I may be finer than I have been in longer than I care to admit."

Lady Gregory finished wiping her eyes. Then she folded her hands in her lap so elegantly Vivian wished she would do it again, just so she could watch the genteel motion, and sat back in her chair.

With a small smile tickling the edges of her lips, the older woman swept a long, lingering look over Vivian. She began at the tips of the serviceable-yet-worn shoes peeking out from beneath the hemline of the seen-better-days brown broadcloth day dress. It was her best dress, a castoff taken out of the bin at the dressmaker's shop. She had done the bodice of a ball gown as payment for the dress. It was the cheapest way

21

she knew to furnish her closet without depleting her purse.

Allowing such an open appraisal should have been disconcerting but she was far too tired to feel anything much. The long ride, debacle upon her arrival and now having to extricate her foot from her mouth had left her entirely drained. She sat, waiting for the commentary that was sure to eventually come.

When it did, it was gentle. Moreover, the words stirred her nearly to tears, they were so kind.

"You are truly something else, Vivian Jane Fox." When her eyes widened at the sound of her middle name in the elegant room, her hostess smiled. "Oh, yes, I know your middle name, my dear. It is no coincidence that my own daughter, Lucie, shares the name. You see, your mother and I were very, very close when we were younger. When we were both newly married our differences seemed to matter less, and the feelings of sisterhood we shared counted more." She sighed, a sound that seemed pulled from her toes.

Waiting for her to continue, Vivian digested the conversation. The nature of her mother's past had never been something they discussed. She imagined it was because they were too busy trying to keep a roof above their heads and food in their bellies. Reminiscences seemed the extravagance of those with less to occupy their hands and nothing but time to waste.

It sounded harsh, but there had not been much about her life that had been easy.

"We are cousins through marriage, you know," Lady Gregory said with a wistful voice. "Not related by blood, but by marriage."

"I did not realize. I always thought…why, Mother

never said…"

"She would not."

Her hostess leaned forward, raised the china pot on the tea tray and held it questioningly between them. With a quick shake of her head, Vivian declined the offer. She looked down into her cup. It was still half full, surely cold by now but she was more interested in the secrets unfolding between them than the promise of a hotter cup of tea.

Lady Gregory filled her own cup, added a splash of cream from the small pitcher on the tea tray and then swished her spoon around in the liquid. The tinkle of sterling on china was musical, a calming interlude in one of the strangest days of Vivian's life.

Sitting back without tasting her tea, the older woman cast a shrewd eye her way. The gesture felt like a test of sorts, so Vivian remained as she was, still and attentive. It did not take long before she saw she survived the assessment.

With classic good looks and a figure that did not announce her age, anyone might have guessed Lord Gregory had robbed the cradle when he chose his wife. The truth was, her third cousin had chosen him and while there were several years separating their ages, she was not all that much younger than he.

"If we are to spend the Season in one another's company, we should not have secrets between us. Do you agree?" Lady Gregory paused, so Vivian nodded. "I am glad we are like-minded. So, that brings us back to the manner by which we are 'family', doesn't it? Apparently your mother did not elaborate when she disclosed our association. I must admit, I am sorry to hear that bit of news. I always…well, I always wished

Regina and I might have the chance to reestablish our friendship. The opening has never presented itself, and I regret that more than I can say."

With a gentle sniff, Lady Gregory stared down at her hands, which were clasped on her lap. Her distress was apparent but Vivian did not know how to comfort her.

"I am sorry you and Mother have not been able to see each other more. I am certain she would love to see you. It would be a pleasurable experience for her, to sit and chat an afternoon away with a treasured friend—ah, treasured *relation*."

Vivian smiled when her hostess looked up at her, and wished she knew what else to say. Too many hours spent with a thimble on her thumb and nearly none in genteel circumstances had left her woefully lacking in the finer points of a lady's sitting room conversation. Surely there was something appropriate she should be murmuring, some platitude or reassurance that would smooth the exchange—but what was it?

She proceeded, emboldened by the lady's wavering smile. She was, evidently, extricating her mother from leaving Lady Gregory—and her sensitive feelings—behind, something for which she was both sad and glad. It was regrettable she had to scramble for excuses.

Why did life have to be so complicated?

"I am sure you and Mother might renew your acquaintance easily. After all, you are related and that does give you a shared history. I am sure you have lost your closeness due only to…" She had done it again—put herself squarely in trouble with her mouth. The meaning beyond her words was clear. Even someone with more hair than wit—which certainly was not true of Lady Gregory—would see what she had been about to say.

Had there been a cupboard nearby, she would have crawled into it and pulled its door closed behind her.

Her hostess acknowledged the rest of the statement with a tight smile.

"You are right, my dear. Completely and utterly correct, there is no denying it—even if you are too well-mannered to finish the statement." She swept a hand at their surroundings, and then dropped it back on to her lap. "Regina and I married into different situations, it is true. She married my cousin Walter, who turned out to be a cad while I, of course, married well. I have always regretted Regina's choice of husband, and have never once wished to trade places with her. No, it is the sad truth that my cousin, your father, could charm the bark off an elm tree but could not manage his affairs any more ably than the tree might have done. Oh dear! I hope I am not offending you, speaking thusly about your father?"

"No offense taken. I am certain you are telling the truth. Besides, since you knew my father and I do not have any memory of him, surely your insights about the kind of man he was—or was not—are much more worthy than any fabrications I might attribute to him. Please, go on. I am interested in hearing all you are willing to share. Mother never speaks of him or of their time together."

A huff of distaste, so unexpected coming from the refined woman seated across from her.

"I should say not. Why would she, when he turned out to be so much less than she hoped? He disappointed us all so much. I am supremely embarrassed that Walter

Fox and I share the same heritage. He was, no matter how much I hate to say so, a rotten branch on an otherwise-healthy family tree." She pulled a lace-edged handkerchief from the cuff of her dress and wiped her brow. "More ghastly, your poor mother had to fall in love with him, and then find herself on her own with a baby. He took everything, every single bit of his inheritance, and frittered it away. Walter's one wise move in a lifetime filled with selfishness and poor judgment was to leave you with your mother. I shudder to think of what might have become of you if he had taken it into his fool head to take you along with him when he left!"

Shortly after her father deserted his family, he died of complications following a riding accident. The news had come by letter and was the last time his life had any impact on either Vivian's or her mother's lives. She had been five at the time, old enough to understand that the man she never knew was someone she was not going to know. His death did not upset her any more then than it did now.

"I cannot imagine having been raised by anyone besides Mother. She never gives up hope. I thought she might, when Grant, her second husband and a man I admired greatly, was stricken by influenza during the epidemic. I suppose having to nurse Liam through the illness, and worrying she or I might come down ill, took her through the worst of it. Mother is wonderful— although I do wish she saw fit to fill me in on some of the twists and turns that lie between us."

Lady Gregory reached between their chairs and placed her hand atop Vivian's. She gave a gentle, reassuring squeeze before she sat back.

"That is what I am here for, my dear. You and I shall become fully acquainted, and I shall divulge the secrets your mother has not been able to tell. She will not mind if I do; in fact, I believe her sending you now is due in part to her wanting you to know the truth about your history. Regina knows I will say what she will not. I will be the voice she has kept silent all these years."

"I will appreciate all you can tell me. It is difficult not having all pieces of the puzzle that is a person's past. I have wondered often about what went on when I was young but there never seemed to be the right time to ask. Besides, Mother has been so busy..." She swallowed hard around the lump which had grown in her throat. Her mother toiled day after day and year after year to provide the necessities of life, without once looking for anything for herself. The enormity of her mother's life came as a cold, hard shock and for a while all she could do was sit quietly, trying to take it all in.

"What a tangled mess Mother's life has been." Vivian looked up, catching Lady Gregory watching her closely, and said, "Why, it is a wonder Mother hasn't been in her cups all this time. No one could blame her if she was, that's for certain."

Tension broke when Lady Gregory laughed the notion away. "Oh, my dear, that is preposterous! I have never known your mother to take as much as a sip of anything stronger than ginger tea—and that only when her stomach was in knots. No, she is not the tippling sort which, I suppose for you and your brother, is a very good trait." She stopped, her expression thoughtful. "I do believe, with all my heart, that Regina would not change one instant of her life with you and Liam—not one single, solitary instant. You shall learn, when your time comes, that a mother will do anything at all to keep her children safe. No sacrifice is too large when it is for one's children. I know Regina has not changed so much that she would not agree with me, so don't waste a precious minute thinking your mother's life has been horrid. She has two lovely children to show for her efforts and that, my dear, is something that cannot be trumped."

Her reply died on her lips. A brisk knock on the door, followed by its being pushed inward, stilled her mind.

****

Oliver had not expected to find their visitor in the sitting room. Had he known she was there he would have waited until later to approach his mother. But he entered the room as he usually did, with his thoughts tumbling from his mouth almost before the door was completely open.

"Mother, I wonder if you would care to give me an opinion on something. Will and I have just been discussing—"

With an indulgent shake of her lovely gray head, Mother looked up at him. A small fire crackled merrily in the grate, lending warmth to the room the thick stone walls did not provide. The manor was old, drafty and, unfortunately, often chilly even during the summer months. A week or two in July was just about the only time when hearths stood empty.

There was a serenity about his mother these days. It gave her a glow and made her look years younger, almost as youthful as he remembered her being during his childhood. Now that Father's health had improved

28

and Lucie was married to Nick, she seemed at peace with everyone and everything. He knew her relaxed attitude was also due in great measure to his being restored to health. His parents did not know the full extent of his madness and illness but they had seen enough to know it was a terrible time.

"Pardon me! I did not realize you were not alone, Mother."

"Evidently." With a smile, his mother reached a hand up to him.

It never crossed Oliver's mind not to take it, so he took a few steps into the room, took his mother's hand in his own and leaned down. Brushing a gentle kiss across her silky skin, he murmured, "Mother." Then, straightening, he stared down into her eyes and attempted to gauge how she felt. She was not as young as she once was, despite her renewed vigor, and he worried about her. Sometimes he wondered if everyone's concern over Father's heart and his "vapors" deflected interest from Mother's health. However, when she smiled up at him she looked in fine form, so he said, "You look well this afternoon. I see having someone here to keep you company has already done you some good."

Manners had been hammered into him from the time he wore leading strings. When his mother took her hand from his, he turned to the guest and bowed. "Miss Fox. How pleasant to see you again."

She remained seated, inclining her head to acknowledge his words. "And you, as well."

Will had come into the room with him, and now bowed to both women in turn. "Lady Gregory. Miss Fox."

29

"William, have you met my cousin's daughter?"

"Not officially. We, ah, we passed each other in the front drive upon the lady's arrival."

Leave it to Will to be so tactful. Oliver fought the twitch of a smile. It was his way, to fit seamlessly into every situation.

"Well, then let me properly introduce you. Vivian, this is William Fulbright. He is Oliver's...hmm..." Turning with a vexed expression pulling her mouth into a straight line, she said, "Will, you are not a valet any longer. You are not just an ordinary household servant. You are more—goodness, we all know you are like family to us, my dear man. But really, what are you? Is there a title I should apply to your introductions from this point onward?"

Oliver smirked at his friend, but gentled his grin for his mother's benefit. "Will is my right-hand man, Mother. It is the truth, and the label fits, I think. What do you say? Does the reference suit him?"

She cast a thoughtful stare upon Will, tapping a fingertip against her cheek as if assessing the number of table scarves in the upstairs linen cupboard. Then, looking from one to the other, she gave a decisive nod.

"Yes, I do think it suits William perfectly." Her hostess's demeanor returned, and she gave her full attention to the waiting guest once again. "As I was saying; this is William Fulbright, Oliver's right-hand man. William, may I present Miss Vivian Fox of Stropshire."

Will bowed so low he looked ready to fall over onto his nose. Just when Oliver thought that might really happen, he straightened. "I am delighted to make your acquaintance, Miss Fox. How long will we have the pleasure of your company?"

"Why, she is staying the entire Season." Mother clapped her hands like a child given a chocolate. The exuberance made Oliver grin even more broadly. How wonderful to see his mother this excited. It occurred to him that perhaps they should have visitors more frequently. He had not known how deeply Mother felt the emptiness created by Lucie's leaving.

Mother pulled William right into the thick of things, giving Oliver a chance to get his thoughts in order. Their guest's sudden appearance had turned the household topsy-turvy, and all in a matter of hours. He knew his mother observed his attitude toward Miss Fox, so he concentrated on being cordial but not effusively friendly.

It was hard to believe that one tiny female could bring such drastic change with her but, strange or not, Miss Fox had done just that. His mother tittered like a schoolgirl and Will dipped and bobbed like some overactive puppet on strings, and all the chatter and laughter in the room brought the noise level higher than it had been in ages.

For her part, Vivian became animated as Will peppered her with polite questions about her home, family and the journey between Stropshire and London. Her face lit up when she spoke of her mother and brother, and it was apparent she loved them dearly. No one made any reference to the family's impoverished station, of course, and she did not offer any information about their living situation other than to say they occupied a flat.

Oliver wondered what flats in Stropshire looked like. Even during his darkest days, during his mental illness, he had never seen any of the less prosperous areas. He knew of their existence, of course, but he had never observed anyplace, or anyone, below his means.

Caught up listening to the fast-paced conversation, he had almost forgotten that he had come to pose a question.

Turning to face him, Mother asked, "You wanted my opinion on something, didn't you? What is it you need to know? Surely it cannot be anything too terribly important, or you would have gone in search of your father and not me."

She giggled—she actually giggled. Oliver could not help himself—his mouth hung open when he heard the sound.

It was a joke, of course. Anything and everything having to do with the manor or the people housed within—be they family members, houseguests or servants—came under Lady Gregory's meticulous care. Her husband took charge of running the stables and overseeing the estate, but the issues involved in running the household had never been, and probably never would be, his jurisdiction.

Lady Gregory was the one to seek when an important decision—or even a minor one—regarding the manor was in the air.

The sitting room door opened wide, pushed so forcefully the door handle banged against the plaster wall behind it. This was not the first time the handle had met the wall; a small indentation in the space testified to the fact.

Lord Gregory, pipe in hand and trailing a thin plume of gray smoke behind him, entered. He laughed as he crossed the room. When he reached his wife, he leaned down and brushed a kiss across her temple.

"Why, I thought I heard a party in here." His ruddy complexion, round cheeks and wispy white hair made him look like Father Christmas. "It is unthinkable, that you would throw a party without inviting me. Why, I feel entirely left out."

"We are just welcoming Vivian." Lady Gregory nodded to the young woman, who looked delighted to be the center of attention. "You remember my cousin Regina, don't you? This is her daughter. Vivian has come to spend the Season with us, darling."

With less bluster than he had shown when he entered, Lord Gregory went to the visitor. He took her hand in his, leaned down and touched her knuckles to his lips. "Why, my dear, I would know you anywhere." He straightened. "You are lovely, and have your father's remarkable purple eyes. They are, I believe, simply spectacular in such a lovely face. Wait until Lucinda sees you. She will be tickled to see those eyes again! When will we see Lucinda next, dear?"

Lady Gregory clapped her hands a second time. "Tomorrow afternoon. We are invited to a lawn party at Waltham Hall. Lucinda's daughter-in-law, Lady Blakely, says she is 'in the mood' for merrymaking." She rolled her eyes, looking quite comical. "And we all know that when Claire is 'in the mood' for something, she gets it. Now do not let me give you the impression she is spoiled or even pampered, Vivian. You shall meet her, and form your own opinions. I look forward to hearing your impressions, not just regarding Claire but about the rest of our set. It is always refreshing to take an account from a fresh perspective." Then, she caught her husband's gaze and said, "Tomorrow, one o'clock. And I completely agree—Lucinda is going to be agog when she gets a look at these lovely lavender eyes."

"Hmmph." Lord Gregory drew deeply on his pipe. "One o'clock, eh? I shall count the hours until the event, then. Surely there will be some fuss when Lucinda sees we have Regina's daughter with us. Remarkable...simply remarkable, those eyes..." He turned to Oliver and said, "Don't you agree, son? Aren't these the most amazing eyes you have ever seen?"

Chapter 3

Sleep was an elusive bedfellow, despite the silkiness of the sheets that covered the most comfortable bed Vivian had reclined—because she did not sleep more than a wink or two—upon. It did not matter that the soft pillow slip beneath her cheek reminded her of a mother's caress. And the soothing hiss and pop of the low fire burning in the grate did not lull her into dreamland.

She tossed and turned like a cork bobbing in a rough sea, and when the first fingers of sunlight crept through the slit in the draperies at the windows she was exhausted. She did not need a looking glass to know there were bags beneath her bloodshot eyes.

How in the world could she possibly get a minute's rest when day followed night? And as surely as dawn would arrive, so would the dreaded lawn party.

Oh, it was not the event itself to blame for the restless night. The prospect of merrymaking—and at a lawn party, no less—excited her. Or it would have, had she anything suitable to wear. The only dress marginally good enough for being seen in had been worn yesterday. Now she wished there had been two frocks among the castoffs.

What she would not give for a more promising wardrobe. Elegant, fashionable clothes had never been an extravagance Vivian could afford. Truthfully, she had never acutely felt the loss. Creating items of beauty had been enough to satisfy any craving she had for fabulous clothing.

Now, however, all those feelings of satisfaction were swept away. She wanted to fit in to the Gregory family's social scene. Her serviceable garments would have everyone believing she was a party-crasher rather than an invited guest. Or, rather, the guest of an invited guest.

Vivian was not one to believe people divided by social and economic conditions were all that much dissimilar. People were people—her mother had hammered that into her head for as long as she could recall.

Still, wearing her rescued castoff and everyone else, including the household staff, garbed in the height of fashion was an unfortunate situation.

What to do?

The possibilities—what few there were—tumbled through her mind like small stones being swept along in a creek's current. She felt each idea as it rattled in her head, was stung every time she discarded a thought as unfeasible.

Before the day had even begun in earnest, Vivian had a headache the size of a lion. It seemed prepared to roar, which would surely set her temples throbbing, so she sat up and pulled the sash of her dressing gown snug about her waist. A table and chairs were set before the largest window in the room. She pulled one of the chairs out and sat heavily, laying her head on the table atop her crossed arms.

A bit of folly, that is what Mother said this jaunt would be. *Folly my foot. I am in well over my head, and sinking fast.*

A knock at the door brought Vivian's head off the table. A maid entered carrying a tray. She dipped a curtsey, and then crossed to the table, placing the tray down without as much as rattling the teacup on its saucer. "Good morning, miss. Would you like me to pull the draperies?"

Her response was not required. The servant went to the window beside the table and pushed the covering back. Sunlight streamed into the room. She watched the maid move from window to window repeating the task until every pane of glass was uncovered and the room bathed in light and warmth.

"There. That's better, isn't it?" The maid came back to the table, standing on the other side with a wide smile. Her gaze darted over Vivian as she introduced herself. "I am Jenny, miss. I am one of the upstairs maids but Lady Gregory thought I might do as your lady's maid while you are with us. I would be honored if you consent to the arrangement. Of course, if I do not suit, there are others who are eager for the position."

Lady's maid? Vivian only had a vague idea of what such a person's duties consisted of. Whatever a "lady's maid" might do for her she was already capable of doing for herself but to say so would be entirely insulting.

Vivian nodded. A lady's maid—good Lord!

"I do not see why you would not suit, Jenny. I, ah, I am grateful to have you assist me in...ah, in my needs." There. That should cover just about everything.

"Very good, miss." Jenny indicated the tray with a nod. "We were not sure whether you might want to take breakfast downstairs or up here in your room."

Breakfast at home usually consisted of a watery cup of tea.

"Where do Lord and Lady Gregory take their morning meal?"

Jenny gave her a small nod, as if her response had been entirely appropriate. "They eat in their rooms, miss. But if you prefer dining downstairs we can accommodate that request. Just say the word and we'll plan on it for every morning ."

"No, that's not necessary. I quite believe I would prefer to eat here. It is such a nice room, and so cheerful in the morning with the sun coming in."

"Yes, miss. Would you like me to serve you? We were not sure what you drink in the morning, so I took the liberty of bringing a pot of hot chocolate as well as a small Brown Betty. The tea is Earl Grey, if you are wondering."

Tea or chocolate? Goodness, but she had fallen out of her ordinary world into a magical existence. It was almost too grand to bear.

Swallowing laughter, Vivian eyed the tray. There were, as Jenny said, two hot pots on its surface as well as several assorted covered dishes, a creamer and a jam pot.

"I can serve myself, thank you."

"Very well." With a bob, the maid headed for the door. She stopped midway, turned back and said, "Miss?"

She could not wait to dive into the contents of the tray but she reined in her enthusiasm and said, "Yes?"

"Lady Gregory sent a note with your tray. It is right there, beside the tea cup."

"Thank you, Jenny."

She waited until the maid left the room before ripping open the beige envelope. Inside, there was a single sheet of heavy vellum paper.

Dear Vivian,

I hope your first night at Willowbrook Manor was a pleasant, restful one. I am told by past guests that the beds are comfortable and, being that we are so isolated from neighbors, the atmosphere quiet. I hope you will find that the case. We do so want you to feel at home here.

It occurred to me that you might not have anticipated being summoned so quickly to a social engagement, and may not be prepared for such. I had hoped you and I might do a bit of shopping, as well as employ the modiste who does most of my clothes, before we began the round of seasonal entertainments. Unfortunately that does not seem to be in our cards. I apologize for not being able to accommodate your needs in the way I wished to do.

If you do not mind terribly (and I pray you do not) there is a solution to this bumblebroth. You occupy my daughter Lucie's old room. I had it readied for you because Lucie always loved it, and I hoped you would as well. More to the point, now that Lucie is married and mistress of her own home, she has taken most of her belongings from the room. There were, however, a modest number of gowns and frocks which she left behind because they needed to be let out. After seeing your willowy, graceful figure it occurs to me that you might find these few garments just your size. Please feel free to take any that might suit your needs. Lucie will not mind in the least. Most of the dresses have never been worn, and most have matching shoes, pelisses and fans. There are also fichus, bonnets and other fripperies in the big closet beside the chest of drawers. Please rummage to your heart's content, use anything that pleases you and, most of all, please forgive me for not having the foresight to stall social engagements until after our shopping spree.

I am so glad you are here, my dear. I pray we become as close as true blood relatives.

Please let Jenny know if there is anything you need. She is yours for the duration of your stay.

Very sincerely,
Ethel Jane

A closet with dresses. Her night terrors had been for naught!

As she rose from the table Vivian took a large bite from a warm orange scone. Its buttery pastry melted in her mouth as she dashed across the room and flung open the closet door.

Oh, good Lord! I have died and gone to Heaven!

****

The drive to Waltham Hall was nothing like the ride to Willowbrook Manor had been. The Gregory carriage was spacious, their horses a practiced team whose hoof beats hardly rocked the conveyance one bit. Instead of dust and mildew filling Vivian's lungs, she inhaled the sweet scent from the covered basket the cook had sent along in case anyone wanted a morsel during their ride.

She could not think of eating. A herd of butterflies frolicked in her middle. She laid a calming hand over her midsection, but the butterflies paid it no mind. She swallowed hard, hoping to discourage them from flying right out her mouth.

"Are you all right, my dear?" Lady Gregory's solicitous nature pushed the fluttery feeling entirely away. When Vivian nodded, it was the truth. She was fine. "Good. I worry we are taxing you. While we are used to the hustle and bustle of Town, you are not. Do not hesitate to say if we are too much, all right?"

"Fiddlesticks." Lord Gregory winked. Seated as he was beside his wife, Vivian was the only one who saw his action. "Vivian is a young lady, darling. She has come all the way from Stropshire to taste some of our fun. I doubt we can run her ragged. It is more likely that you and I will be the ones worn to a shred. We are old, and she is young. She probably wonders when the fun will begin, and when she will be able to lose the two old fogies her mother saddled her with for the Season." He leaned forward. There was ample space between the two seats, so the duke had to reach out to pat her arm. Sitting back, he said, "That's it, my dear, isn't it? You are conjuring schemes to scamper from the two of us, aren't you? Do not be shy; I cannot blame you a whit. If I were in your position I would do the same."

Horror turned her throat as dry as the Sahara desert. Vivian felt the color drain from her face as her hands turned clammy. How could they believe she wanted to get away from them? Why, she had just arrived and already knew she would love to spend every night of the rest of her life in the cozy bed back in her room at the manor.

"No! I-I—good Lord, I definitely am not thinking anything of the sort. Lord Gregory, please forgive me if I have given such a bad impression. Why, I never—"

A large sigh escaped Lady Gregory's lips. She scowled, turned to face her husband and said, "What goes on in that head of yours? Goodness, look at how you have managed to get our guest in such a twist—and so quickly! We are used to your silly pranks—she is not." She faced Vivian again and spread one hand, palm up, to her. "Look at how you've upset her. She believes you, you and your practical jokes."

Lord Gregory's eyes stopped twinkling. He looked chagrined, his moustache drooping low over his lips and his pipe forgotten in his hand.

"You are right. I am incorrigible, frightening her with my hijinks and it is entirely improper." He looked from wife to guest and back to his wife again. With a sigh, he asked, "When will I learn, darling? Not everyone enjoys a joke as well as I do."

Vivian hated seeing him so deflated. "I love a joke! Truly, I do. I just did not realize…well, let us just say I am not as adept at seeing humor as you are at dispensing it. Mother says I am as serious as an old toad sometimes, and I do believe she is right."

His humor restored, the duke chuckled. "An old toad? You? My dear, you could never be anything of the sort. Why, I could see you a graceful damselfly or perhaps a hummingbird, but never a toad. Why, what a preposterous notion!"

****

Waltham Hall lay just outside London proper, and retained many features similar to Lord and Lady Gregory's residence. The estate was not as big, and the edifice not so grand, but it was far more luxurious than anything Vivian was used to seeing.

They arrived just in time for lunch. Serving tables were set up near Lady Blakely's rose garden. They were laden with sumptuous offerings, heavenly scents being borne on the warm summer breeze.

Vivian's stomach rumbled and her mouth watered. She surveyed the selections, completely overwhelmed by the sheer volume of food. Surely this could not all be meant for just one meal?

None of the other guests looked startled by the fare, or its staggering amount. Apparently the serving dishes, platters and heaping bowls were not out of the ordinary for such events.

After greeting Lady Blakely, and having been made to promise to amble through her hostess's prized roses at some point during the day, she had lost her sponsors. They had disappeared into the crowd while she and Lady Blakely had been discussing the merits of different shades of rose petal—their hostess favored pink while Vivian had a mind for red—and had not reappeared since.

Striped tents scattered about the lawn, with seating in loosely arranged clusters beneath every tree and near all the fountains, statues and stone walls dotting the area. The effect was studied casual, and very welcoming. It would have been pleasant to pass the afternoon in the space in solitude, a sanctuary far above any an ordinary park would provide.

A uniformed maid appeared by Vivian's elbow.

She walked on silent feet, cushioned by the lush green grass.

"Luncheon, miss?"

Vivian jumped. She whirled about to face the young woman.

"Pardon?"

"Sorry, miss. I did not mean to give you a fright." A tiny apologetic smile. "Forgive me, please. It is only that I saw you standing here by yourself, and wondered if you might be ready for lunch. I would be happy to serve you."

As if on cue, her stomach growled. The maid pretended not to notice, but Vivian could not see how she did not hear. The sound was loud and insistent.

In her excitement over finding a roomful of beautiful dresses, she had neglected her breakfast tray. It had looked delectable but the pretty fabrics and buttery-soft slippers had enticed her more than the cook's offerings.

"I would love that, thank you."

The maid inclined her head. "Would you like me to fill a plate for you, or would you care to choose for yourself?"

Passing up the chance to get a closer look at the marvels spread on the serving tables was something she could not do.

"I would rather choose."

"As you wish, miss. This way, then." The servant led the way to the first table, picked up a silver-edged dinner plate and waited. When Vivian did not move, she said, "I am ready. Just tell me what looks good to you and I will see that you get a taste. Anytime you are ready, then."

Enthusiasm to sample a bit of everything spurred her on. Every dish looked appetizing, even those she did not recognize. Welsh rarebit, roast beef, puddings of all sorts, vegetables she had never heard of—let alone tasted—and a dozen other delectable aromas captivated her. All she had to do was smile when a dish lid was raised or nod when the maid's hand hovered above a serving spoon.

It did not take long for the fancy white plate to be filled. When it could hold no more, she turned to view her seating options.

"Where do you wish to sit?"

Since she did not know anyone besides the Gregorys—who were still absent from sight—she decided it best she sit by herself. Indicating a small table in the shade of a sprawling elm tree, Vivian grabbed a napkin and flatware as she passed the last serving table and headed for one of the folding chairs tucked beneath the table's edge. The maid followed, and when Vivian sat down she placed the plate on the table.

"Anything else, miss?"

"No, thank you. I believe this will do for now." Vivian dropped the snowy linen napkin onto her lap, picked up the fork and smiled. "Yes, I think I'm set for a while."

Chapter 4

Lady Blakely cut a swath through her milling guests like Moses parting the Red Sea. No one hesitated when she approached, moving a step either forward or back to allow her unimpeded movement from one end of the wide, rolling lawn to the other. Then, like a flock of geese on a lake, those assembled dipped, nodded and bobbed ever-so slightly, a dramatic show of respect for one of London's greatest hostesses.

Feeling a bit like a tail on a kite, Vivian followed, taking care not to let too much distance show between her and Lady Blakely. She feared that just as the Sea closed after Moses, so might the crowds converge following the Lady's passage.

No one had joined Vivian for lunch. She had garnered quite a number of semi-covert glances and a couple of outright stares but no one had ventured over to her little table beneath the tree. It was a shame, really. The spot had been ideal, and she would have stayed right there even after a maid collected her empty plate and discarded flatware. It might have been nice to inhabit the spot for the entire afternoon, just watching people and getting a sense of the unfamiliar world in which she currently found herself.

Lady Blakely had other ideas for her, however. Not long after she had consumed the last delicious bite of lunch, her hostess appeared from behind and introduced herself. When she stood and curtsied, Vivian spied Lord and Lady Gregory a short distance away. They occupied an even more secluded dining table. They waved, but Vivian kept her attention on the woman before her.

It seemed inconceivable that someone so tiny could command such interest. Not having an insider's view of London's elite did not keep Vivian from realizing that the petite woman with almost childlike features moved social mountains with the wave of a hand. When she told Vivian she intended to introduce her to "some bright young minds" she did not doubt it.

When Lady Blakely stopped it was so abrupt that Vivian nearly collided with her. If the other woman feared she might be tumbled to the grass she did not show it. Instead, she gave one general nod to the small knot standing beside a marble fountain. Three nods and a bow quickly acknowledged their arrival.

With a wave of her hand, Lady Blakely made the introductions. She began with the woman standing closest to them, a pretty, plump redhead who looked glad to be diverted from whatever had been going on before their appearance.

"Miss Miranda Spencer, of London."

Miss Spencer bobbed, the long ribbon of curls beside her right cheek falling forward as she lowered. Straightening, she pushed the errant locks behind the shoulder of the robin's egg blue dress she wore and said, "My pleasure."

Before Vivian could do more than half-nod, Lady Blakely moved the airborne hand to the next woman. In direct contrast to the first, she had a barely-concealed scowl on her face. Thick black eyebrows were so tightly drawn together they looked like a black caterpillar marching across her forehead, and the dark curls beside her ears were so heavily sprayed they seemed cast in stone.

"Miss Rebecca Hastings, also of London."

Miss Hastings barely bent her knees, and her nod was sharp enough to slice bread.

Again before Vivian could properly react, Lady Blakely turned to the final young woman.

For her part, she curtsied so deeply and well in advance of her name being said that when their hostess announced, "Miss Eloise Smythe, of London and..." Lady Blakely sniffed, the sound so low it was almost inaudible. Nonetheless, it was a sniff, and standing nearly shoulder to shoulder with the woman, Vivian heard it. "Paris."

Someone with more flair than most.

A furtive head to toe glance at Miss Smythe's rising confirmed the suspicion. Her dress was the palest pink silk with an underskirt just a shade darker. The contrast was stunning, and the embroidered hemline and low-cut, ribbon-trimmed neckline was surely a one-of-a-kind creation intended solely for its owner. She had sewn enough gowns to know by sight that the one Miss Smythe wore had not been made in London.

The reason for the sniff, she thought. Not unreasonable, really. Who wouldn't want a Parisian wardrobe?

There was no time to waste thinking. Lady Blakely's hand gestured to the only man in the group. She favored him with a warm smile that the ladies had not seen.

"Lord Stuart Bailey, the Duke of Chichester. He is,

I shall tell you right off, one of London's most eligible bachelors. A great catch and an expert with the horses. The ladies, too, I hear."

"You flatter me, Lady Blakely." The duke's voice was velvety smooth, with a teasing tone that made their hostess titter. When he turned his attention on Vivian she saw more than a casual interest in his eyes. His gaze rested on her face for a long moment before he bowed low, giving a grand sweep of his leg that sent her heart pounding madly in her chest. No man had made such a gesture to her before and it inspired emotions she had not thought she owned.

This is what it must feel like to be the Queen.

"I am delighted, Miss..." The duke rose and looked askance to Lady Blakely.

"Miss Vivian Fox, of Stropshire. She is staying with Lord and Lady Gregory for the Season," Lady Blakely said, her introductory hand finally before Vivian.

"It is an absolute pleasure, Miss Fox."

The duke's attention tied her tongue in knots, so she just nodded and dropped into a general curtsey. She hoped it covered all elements of propriety.

With a satisfied nod, their hostess walked away. The crowd opened, then closed, around her and before a moment passed she was out of sight.

Evidently they had walked in on a hearty discussion, because as soon as she departed the exchange resumed. No inquiries were made of her and since participation in the conversation did not seem necessary—or desired—Vivian kept her own council. She was, however, all ears.

Miss Hastings glowered more fiercely without

Lady Blakely's presence. She was in sharp contrast to Miss Smythe's smiling countenance when she hissed, "Stupid!"

Vivian's eyes opened wide. Even in baser circles, one rarely maligned another without harsh provocation.

Paris played no part in Miss Smythe's reaction. It was pure Londoner when she snorted her derision. "Pish posh! You cannot know what you are talking about. You have never been anywhere and have not done anything extraordinary—that is, unless you count curling your hair and combing your eyebrows astonishing endeavors."

She would have laughed aloud had she not feared it would hasten the discussion's end. Apparently Miss Smythe was more than a Paris powder puff!

"Ladies, is this really necessary? What will Miss Fox think of us, sniping at each other this way?" Miss Spencer smoothed a shaky hand down the front of her dress. Her voice trembled when she added, "Besides, you both know I hate arguments. You know how they unsettle me. Please, let us stop this foolishness. It does not matter who bakes the fluffiest biscuits. French or English bakers, what does it matter? It is not as if any of us are going to test them, anyhow. We all know how bad biscuits are for our waistlines."

Vivian did not point out that she had eaten two light-as-air biscuits just a short time ago. Had she not been so full she might have polished off another.

"Hmmph!" It was a deadly sound, a gooseflesh-producing growl. It was the only reply Miss Hastings offered.

"So true." Miss Smythe smiled sweetly. "Miranda does have a point. We should drop the topic at once.

We must have more stimulating things to speak of...Your Grace, weren't you about to tell us about that sporty new conveyance parked over there? I could have sworn I saw you drive up in it."

Vivian noticed Miss Smythe step closer to the duke. When he turned to look at the carriage, the woman by his side did not attempt to hide her interest in him. Staring openly at his profile, she threaded her fingers together before her waist.

The duke turned his attention back to the ladies. He pushed his fingers through his sandy-colored hair. Despite his touch, the waves did not become mussed and Vivian wondered if he and Miss Hastings used the same hair fixative.

She could not stop the grin from forming on her face. The duke caught sight of it and, like a small boy seeking his nanny's approval, asked, "Do you like my curricle, Miss Fox?"

What could she say?

"It is, ah, very pretty."

He threw his head back and laughed. Heat rose on her cheeks, and she realized her mistake almost as soon as it was out.

"Pretty? Miss Fox, I have never heard anyone call such a sporty little rig pretty before. You are a true Original. Pretty, indeed. Well, I do thank you for the compliment. I can tell now that you do not have an interest in carriages."

"That is not so." Vivian spoke without considering her words before they left her mouth. "I am very much interested in your..."

"Curricle."

"Yes, your curricle. In fact, I am so excited to see

your sweet little carriage that I cannot help but think it must be like flying to ride in it." She sighed, her gaze lingering on the vehicle's black leather seats. They looked soft.

"Really?" Surprise tinged the duke's voice.

"Oh, yes. I would love to take a ride in your, ah, curricle."

Grabbing her by the hand and pulling her after him, the duke said, "If it is a ride you want, Miss Fox, it is a ride you shall get!"

The ride home in Lord and Lady Gregory's carriage was much more sedate than the jaunt around Waltham Hall's grounds with Lord Stuart Bailey.

He had insisted she call him Stuart, and had been as bold as to kiss her cheek when he returned her to the party. Vivian hoped no one had seen the gesture. It was not something she intended to let happen again. The duke was kind enough, and he had a mad sense of humor, which kept her laughing the whole time they rode the grounds. But he was not the kind of man she could take seriously. His genial outlook was admirable but there was a sense about him that indicated he did not have a single responsible bone in his body. The fact that the curricle was new, a replacement for last year's model, and that the older one had been smashed against a tree during one wild midnight ride did not impress her. The waste and disregard for property annoyed her, and although she kept a bland expression on her face she had no desire to go riding with the duke in the future.

"Did you enjoy yourself, Vivian?" Lady Gregory had her head on her husband's shoulder, and he had one arm wrapped around her. Their comfort in each other's company was an inspiration. It was what she wanted for herself, a man with whom she could feel absolutely at ease.

"Very much, thank you."

"Oh, you are welcome, my dear. I am glad you found the affair amusing. I admit, last night when I realized we have not gone on a proper shopping trip yet I was afraid you would not agree to go today. Your adaptability under duress is an admirable trait, and I appreciate your forgiving my oversight. I am glad you found something suitable among Lucie's things. To tell the truth, that dress looks much nicer on you than it would have ever looked on Lucie. Don't you agree, darling?"

The duke had been snoring quietly but when his wife asked the question he opened one eye, looked to Vivian's side of the carriage, and then closed the eye. "Much nicer. More the figure for it, really. Lucie can be a bit..."

His wife shushed him. "He is right, you know. Our Lucie has quite the hourglass figure. She is not nearly as slender as you. She is not chubby, mind you; she is just not willowy and slim. That neckline would have been unfortunate on her. No, it is much better on you, my dear. Much."

"I cannot thank you for your generosity. I have never worn anything this lovely."

"You need not thank me. It is a delight having you with us. I feel more at home now that I am not the only woman in residence. I do so miss our Lucie...it is kind of you to take up where she has left off. And I know you will love her when you finally meet her, She and Nick should be arriving home tonight from Ireland. He loves to travel, as does our daughter."

"Hmmph!" The duke's moustache quivered in the exhalation accompanying the sound.

Lady Gregory patted his arm affectionately. "There, there, darling. Do not upset yourself. Remember your heart, now." She rubbed her fingers over his knuckles. Their gloves lay on the seat beside them so the action brought a whisper of skin on skin to the space. "My husband does not think women need to travel. He believes traveling the world is the domain of men, and that we females should stay put and keep the home fires burning. What do you think of that?"

The duke opened one eye again. He caught her gaze, and Vivian learned how it felt to be a jackrabbit caught in the hunter's crosshairs. She swallowed hard, searching for a reply that would not offend either Gregory.

The truth. It was the only way to go in this—or any—matter.

"I do not know what I think, honestly. I have never had the opportunity to travel, or even dream of doing so. This trip to London is the furthest I have been from home. It is exciting, and I love the chance to meet new people and see intriguing things—as well as wear pretty dresses and go to parties. I just cannot say definitely, however, that I am either for or against women traveling. That, I believe, is a judgment best left to those with more experience."

"Well done, Vivian." The duke smiled, closing his eyes again. "You should be in Parliament, my dear."

"In any event," Lady Gregory continued, "Lucie and Nick are looking forward to meeting you. I know they want to welcome you personally, and Lucie hopes to spend time taking you to the shops and museums."

"I look forward to it."

The rest of the ride passed in silence. Now and then a snore punctuated the journey but for the most part Vivian was left to sort through her own thoughts.

Oliver was waiting for them. Pacing the front hallway, his hair standing on end and agitation spilling from every pore, he looked ready to scream. His parents hurried to him, flanking him and worriedly peppering him with questions.

"Oliver, are you unwell?" His father asked.

"Did something happen?" Lady Gregory pressed a hand to his forehead. He leaned back, away from her touch. "Did you—you know?"

"Son, are you—"

He disengaged himself and took a step back, plowing his fingers through his already mussed locks. The image of a porcupine came to Vivian's mind but it fled as quickly as it had come. Oliver looked ready to burst, and for a second she feared for her Mother and Liam. Had something awful happened?

"It is not what any of you are thinking," Oliver said with a sigh. "It is bad, but not catastrophic. I am sure you wondered why I did not make it to Waltham Hall this afternoon. I had planned on going to the party after I did the weekly ride about the property. I usually check the cottages and Folly, just to be sure all is well. I know the groundskeepers look after things but it is good, as well, for the owner to keep a hand in."

"Quite so, son." Lord Gregory jerked a nod as he reached into his jacket pocket for his pipe tobacco. The pipe was already between his teeth, and he seemed in need of a calming diversion.

"Anyhow, all looked fine until I got to the cottage nearest the estate's boundary. The one by the road out of town. Anyhow, when I arrived and checked the lock I knew we had a problem."

In a swirl of fragrant smoke, the duke asked, "A problem? What sort of problem, Oliver?"

"We have been robbed."

Chapter 5

"You are going to hurt yourself—or worse, hurt me—if you do not watch what you are doing." Will sidestepped the foil thrust at him. "Be careful, won't you? That thing is sharp and even if you do not value your vitals, I do mine. I would certainly not like to see my entrails become fertilizer for the grass."

Oliver grinned, and then thrust a second time. This time the sharp instrument sent a vibration through his hand and up into his arm when he connected with his opponent's shoulder.

Had his aim been slightly to the left and his intention been to kill rather than let off steam, Will's blood would likely have splattered the ground at their feet.

"Lucky for you, old man, that I don't mean to skewer you."

Glowering his annoyance when the sharp instrument glanced off him, Will took three rapid steps forward. Oliver saw him coming, and recognized the move as one of the other man's best, but he did not react quickly enough to avoid being struck. When the tip of Will's fencing foil dug into the heavy fabric covering his torso, he knew he must concede. Without the protective vests they both wore, Will would have been victorious. Even now he could, with one bold thrust, send his weapon slicing into Oliver's gut.

Swallowing a passing jolt of alarm, he lowered his foil and nodded his concession.

Instantly Will pulled his weapon back and pointed the tip toward the ground. He did not look pleased by his win.

"It was either kill or be killed," Will growled. Wiping at a rivulet of sweat with the back of one hand, he raised an eyebrow and asked, "Was it your intention to exercise or murder? Clearly we had two separate understandings of the morning's activity."

They walked to the low stone wall that bordered the space where they practiced fencing maneuvers. An elm tree shaded one end. Removing their vests and laying them beside their foils before they sat beside their equipment, they caught their respective breaths in silence.

Finally, Oliver exhaled. It should have brought relief to his racing pulse but it did not. No amount of slow, deep breathing or strenuous exercise could wipe away the unease that occupied the biggest part of his mind.

No one had ever dared to steal—not even an apple from their orchard—from them before now. It was despicable, yes. Worse, it was a betrayal of trust that eroded the very fabric of their existence. The estate was home to all manner of servants, many with families in residence on or near the property. To think that one of them had stolen from his family was almost too much to bear.

"I am sorry." He rubbed a hand along his stubbled cheek. The rasping sound was oddly soothing. "I meant to work off some of this excess energy, not commit murder. I assure you, if I wished your spoon stuck in the wall I would have taken you down a long time ago. No, my friend, perish the thought of your dying. I count on you too much to lose you."

Will shook his head. "That is something, I suppose. I will say that I do not recall you playing so hard in a long, long time. It was as if…"

The past was never far removed, was it? Oliver's debacle was always within memory's grasp and somehow fit snugly into nearly any conversation. His shame over his wrongdoing was also always lying upon his shoulders, heart and conscience.

"I know. I acted as erratically as I did last year, when I nearly lost my mind and you almost paid for my bad behavior with your very life."

"It was the demons." Will's favorite expression for that time. They shared a wry smile, both aware that even the foulest demons could not be held completely responsible for what had transpired.

"Hmm, the demons. That is as good an excuse as any, old man. Still, I am sorry to have fenced like a man possessed. I did not mean to conjure demons, but to escape from them."

"Your father still refuses to contact the constable?"

"He will not hear of it. He will not allow us to send word to his solicitor, either, although I am in agreement with him on that one. It is Mother who wants Mr. Pimm involved. I suppose she just wants *someone* to take the burden from us but really, what can a solicitor do? Until the thief is caught there is no one to hold accountable. If Father will not listen to reason and alert the authorities, it falls to me to find the culprit."

There was no other way that he could fathom to solve the dilemma. Someone had to come to justice, and if that meant he had to track the responsible person down, then that was what he was going to do.

A suspect had already come to mind. He hated to think it could be possible but it was logical.

"You know I will help in any way I can." Will looked up at the clear blue sky. The sun was nearly at its apex, and the day much warmer now than when they first grabbed their fencing equipment. He turned his attention on Oliver, and with a serious tone said, "We have been through so much already. I do not imagine hunting down one brazen thief can be anything to worry over. By now you have most likely got someone in mind, if I know you. Tell me, what are your thoughts on this messy bit of business?"

It seemed sacrilege to say it but there was no holding back with Will. They had few, if any, secrets from one another.

Searching for a way to be tactful without diminishing his supposition, he said, "I have given this a great deal of thought. In fact, I hardly slept last night, I was so caught up in thinking about the situation. As far as I can tell, the cottage was fine last Thursday. I checked it then and did not see anything amiss. Certainly the door lock was secure and there were no broken windows in the place. Talbot rode past on Sunday, with his wife. They went picnicking after church services. He swears he did not notice anything out of the ordinary, and I believe him."

Rennie Talbot had been in his father's employ as a groundskeeper for over a decade. He and his wife lived in one of the estate apartments set aside for servant usage. The apartments were situated in a north wing of the manor, useful for keeping staff close at hand yet on their own as well. It did not seem possible that Talbot would not tell the truth. He had no reason to lie.

"I do, too. Rennie and Leila are good people. Their Sunday picnics are a habit with them, and I know they ordinarily go to a spot near the cottage. Closer to the little brook that is out that way, I think, is where they actually spread their blanket. I have heard Leila say that the brook is music enough to make Rennie fall asleep, and that she is used to his napping while she reads a book. Sounds pretty comfortable to me. Don't you think?"

It did not typically fall to the lord of the manor to find a point in his servants' lives to envy, but Oliver did feel a twinge in this case. The familiarity between the Talbots, as well as the handful of other married couples living on the estate, was enviable.

Someday I will lie on a blanket and doze while my wife reads, Oliver thought with a wistful pang.

He straightened his spine. Sitting on a stone wall was great for a temporary rest but taxed the back if done for any length of time. He jumped to the ground, stretched and nodded his agreement.

"The Talbots seem a reputable source of information. We are agreed on that." Oliver picked up his vest and foil. He had reasoned the matter out in his head several times but hearing it aloud only made him surer he had a lead in the theft. "The robbery had to occur between Sunday and Monday, then. The cottage is nearest the road, which is only sporadically traveled. Most of the time it is desolate, so anyone might easily sneak onto the property, to the cottage and…well, let us just say it would be the most likely way to steal something from the place."

"Anyone, then, is capable of carrying out your plan. Everyone is a suspect, if it is that easy to accomplish the deed."

Will gathered his equipment and the pair began to walk slowly back to the manor. The heat on Oliver's head did not sufficiently chase the chill from his heart. If what he suspected was true, there were going to be people who were hurt by the news. In particular, his parents, and he hated the idea of doing one thing to upset either of them. He had done enough of that in his lifetime already, and had not atoned nearly enough to repay the sadness he had brought to their lives.

"Not everyone. We need only suspect those who traveled the road on either Sunday or Monday. Actually, we can narrow that down to Sunday night or Monday."

Will snapped his fingers, turning so quickly he caught the shin of Oliver's buckskins with the tip of his foil. The steel punctured the deerskin but, fortunately, did not pierce Oliver's.

"Now who is trying to kill whom?" Oliver, knowing he was not injured, kept walking.

"Sorry! It is just that I wonder how you can be so sure it happened by Monday. Why not Tuesday morning? You don't check the cottages until late in the day Tuesday. Yesterday you were early because of the lawn party but you are usually much later. That is neither here nor there, in any case. It still could have happened yesterday morning."

"I don't think so. Monday night there was a bit of a breeze, remember? I found leaves inside on the floor, and surmise they got blown in during the night. So that leaves Sunday night or Monday. And, while I hate to say it, we know of at least one carriage that went that way on Monday, don't we?"

Will stopped short. He turned, a look of astonishment on his face. "You don't mean…?"

They were within shouting distance of the house. Lord and Lady Gregory waved from their position at one of the tables set out on the broad stone terrace. Oliver waved with his free hand.

"That is exactly what I mean." They were too far from anyone to be overheard but he spoke softly nonetheless. It seemed the fitting thing to do, considering what they discussed. "The only one I know of who passed that way on Monday was our new houseguest."

"I cannot believe it. Miss Fox seems so-so-so—"

Watching Will sputter would have been comical had they not been discussing such a serious offense.

"Innocent?" The word tasted sour. When Will nodded, he could not look directly into his eyes. He began walking toward the terrace, and was pleased Will did the same. Just before they reached his parents, Oliver said, "In most crime novels the one who seems the most innocent is the criminal."

****

Now that is the look of a woman in love, Vivian thought as she watched Lady Lucinda Jane Grayson pour a second cup of tea from the pot that had just been brought into the library. She refilled Miranda's cup without asking, and then wordlessly held it out to her. Vivian shook her head, declining the offer and watched the light sparkle on the duchess's wedding ring as she placed the pot in the center of the table. It was the second pot, the first having been depleted by the trio over introductory small talk. Now that they were getting down to more personal topics a fresh pot of tea seemed necessary, and Vivian was glad for that. She wanted a chance to get better acquainted with both women—even if that meant she had to drink countless cups of tea!

Today Miranda wore a morning dress made of shimmery pale turquoise fabric. Every time she moved, the dress rippled in a way that was all but mesmerizing. The dress's graceful undulations and her fiery red mane, done in all-over ringlets held off the face with a deep turquoise ribbon, made Vivian think of mermaids. The effect was stunning and she could not keep from admiring the look.

"I am so glad you are back from your trip, Lucie." Miranda ran a gentle hand down her skirt. "I missed you."

"And I you." Lucie sipped her tea, a sigh passing through her rosebud lips.

Miranda grinned at Vivian as if they shared a secret. Female companionship was something she had not had much experience with so she loved the feeling of inclusion. She smiled back, her smile growing wider when the other woman winked.

"Judging by that sigh, your trip with His Grace must have proved…satisfactory." A tiny giggle punctuated her words.

Lucie colored slightly and waved her hand through the air. Again the sunlight streaming through the window hit her wedding ring. Rainbows of colors prismed from her finger, making the leather-bound volumes filling the room's bookshelves seem alive.

"You must stop calling Nick that. Honestly, it is

much too formal. Why, you and I are nearly sisters; how can you address the man who will be like a brother to you in no time as 'Your Grace'? You cannot do it, Miranda. Or you either, Vivian. My husband would definitely prefer a more informal address, I am sure of it." At the mention of the duke, Lucie sighed dreamily. "And to answer your question, we did have a pleasant time in Ireland. It all was very satisfactory."

"What was it like? Ireland, I mean." Stropshire had insulated her from the outside world, and while she had never minded that she was inexplicably drawn to hearing more about someplace so far from home.

I could not miss what I did not know, she thought with a twinge. Now I know...will I begin to miss things that I shall never have?

"Oh, Ireland was divine! All moldy old castles, rolling green hills and quaint little villages." Lucie put a hand over her heart. "It was heavenly."

"It sounds like England," Miranda said with a laugh. "You have just turned me off from wanting to see the place. Why, if I travel anywhere it is going to be somewhere that does not remind me of here."

Vivian heard something that sounded strangely like disgust in Miranda's voice and wondered what caused it. She did not have long to guess, since Lucie asked the question she was not bold enough to ask.

"What is wrong with here? I have always loved England, and you have, too." Lucie leaned forward, her eyes filled with concern. "What has changed in my absence to make you sound so sour? It is not like you to act this way."

Vivian shifted in her chair when the redhead's gaze swung her way. She felt as nervy as a long-tailed cat in a roomful of rocking chairs, and wondered which way to dart in order to keep the end of her tail from being squeezed.

"I do not wish to say." Now her tone was a sad one, and it pushed her friend to interrogate her further.

"Don't be such a silly goose. It's obvious something is troubling you." Lucie looked to Vivian for confirmation, and seemed satisfied with a quick nod. "Vivian sees it as well. Come now, tell us what is on your mind. And don't hold back because of our guest. Why, I have spoken to Mother and she is already in love with our dear cousin so it is safe to share your secrets. Besides, she is a relation, and as such is in the family's inner circle. You must not be shy around her. It simply would not do."

It felt like her stomach fell right down into the toes of her borrowed slippers when Miranda glanced at her. Vivian had felt lighthearted when she dropped the rose-patterned dress over her head. Its scooped neckline and tulip sleeves had made her feel like a princess, and when she found the matching slippers, with rosebuds embroidered onto their toes, she had been truly delighted.

Now, however, elation seeped out of her like air from a bellows—in one sharp *whoosh* that made her head spin.

Whatever it is, it seems best to meet this head on.

"Lucie is right. I can see that whatever is bothering you has to do with me." Vivian cleared her throat, trying to push the shakiness from her voice. She swallowed hard, and then asked. "What have I done? Please, tell me so I can make it right."

"You have not done a thing. Well…" Miranda's

cheeks looked like apples and her lower lip quivered as she twisted her fingers in her lap. Her distress was enough to send thoughts for herself scattering. She put a hand on the woman's arm, and spoke softly, the way she did with Liam when he was upset.

"Whatever it is, it is not worth getting yourself distressed over. Is it, Lucie?"

"Of course it isn't. Come, tell us what is wrong so we can address the problem. I know you hate upheaval but there is no denying your discomfort." She put her hand on Miranda's other arm and patted it encouragingly. "Just spill the beans, dear. We are all adults here and together we will find a way out of whatever flap any of us is in. That is it, isn't it? One of us is in a flap, and you are afraid you will hurt our feelings by saying so. I know you well…just spill it, and you will feel much relieved."

Miranda's nod sent her curls bouncing. She looked from one woman to the other, and then said, "It is Vivian."

"What about Vivian?" Lucie asked, shooting her a look that said *Be still and let me uncover the problem.* They had not known each other long but it did not take a lifetime of knowing someone to see such a clear intention.

Now that the truth was out in the open Miranda did not hold back. Her gaze grew hard when she said, "It is not all her fault. It is this world we live in, with its stringent social rules that put every woman at a disadvantage. Why, if we were men we would not be having this discussion."

"But we aren't men, so we must, apparently, have a discussion." Lucie sat back in her chair, looking certain that it was only a matter of time before the mystery of the distress would be unraveled. "What is it, precisely, that we are discussing? I still am in the dark about it, as I am certain poor cousin Vivian is as well."

Miranda balled her hands into fists. "Convention! That is the root of all evil, I daresay. It is what prevents us from behaving as we would like and is what allows others—unconscionable reprobates, I say—to speak ill of us."

"Oh, for heaven's sake. Just spill it already. You have got Vivian at sixes and sevens, and who can blame her? She probably imagines she has insulted the Regent himself, you are going on so. Just say it. What awful deed did my cousin carry out?"

The cream from her tea felt curdled in her stomach. A sour taste rose in her throat, burning the back of her mouth and bringing tears to her eyes. Vivian wished, in that half-second between knowing and not knowing, that she had stayed in Stropshire. At least there she knew when she had stuck her foot in something.

"She *ate*." Miranda sighed, as if the effort of recounting the horror had been too much for her.

"Whatever do you mean...?" Understanding lit Lucie's eyes, and she turned to Vivian and said, the words borne on another sigh, "You ate at the lawn party, didn't you?"

"Of course I ate." Goodness, where she came from no one saw food like had been at the previous day's party. Sheer stupidity, that is what it would have been, for her to pass up the chance to eat her fill. A swell of justification rose within her, so she added, "I sampled nearly everything on the buffet table. It was all quite delicious."

"Everything?"Lucie's eyes grew as round as tea saucers. "You tried everything?"

"She did. Every single dish, from what I hear."

"What do you mean? From what you hear—how is it that you hear anything about what I did or did not eat?" Indignation chased trepidation away in a heartbeat. Whatever could these two be going on about? It did not make any sense at all.

"Oh, by now tongues are wagging, I assure you." Lucie looked amused. "I wager they wagged so fast they were nearly set afire yesterday, even before the party ended. That's the truth, Miranda, isn't it?"

"You know it is. Why, even before I met Vivian I knew she had eaten—all *alone*, no less—beneath a tree near the serving tables. It was the talk of the party."

"*Tsk-tsk-tsk*, Vivian. You have no idea you committed a social blunder, do you? Oh, my dear cousin, I believe I love you already. Why, to think you could actually attend a party and eat your fill without anyone noticing—why, that is such a novel idea I almost wish I had thought of it myself." Lucie steepled her fingers, placing her elbows on the arms of her chair and staring thoughtfully across the table. It did not take an interpreter to see she considered her next words carefully before she spoke them.

Their tea had been long forgotten. By now it would be cold if any of them cared to taste it.

She waited, holding her breath while the other two women exchanged knowing looks.

"I see we shall have to educate you in the ridiculous ways of Society." Lucie smiled broadly, her eyes twinkling as if she looked forward to the job. "It will not do to have you appear to be such a green girl. It is no wonder you are not aware of the silly intricacies of polite society. There is no example of such in Stropshire, so how could you know what is expected and what is expressly forbidden to a young woman of some social standing?"

Vivian shook her head wearily. "Eating is forbidden?"

"Only in view of those who might think you too robust," Miranda answered. "Eating in moderation is fine, but to heap your plate the way you did and eat as much as two hansom cab drivers is out of the question. It does not look good, and does make you seem a bit hoydenish. A lady eats small, dainty amounts—all things in moderation. That is, I believe, the key to the mealtime situation."

"Agreed." Lucie shrugged."When I am with family or friends I may eat a third—or even a fourth—scone if I wish, but I would never dream of doing so before any I might wish to impress. Delicate; that is something a woman wishes to portray at all times."

"Delicate." She tucked the word into one corner of her mind, although it was entirely unnecessary. After today's conversation she would never make the same mistake she had made yesterday. No one would accuse her of being hoydenish again. Ever!

"That's correct." Now that the initial disclosure was behind them, Miranda warmed to the exchange. Her hands were no longer fisted, and she waved them in the air around her head for emphasis. "A woman is, above all else, restrained. It is something we have been taught from the time we wore leading strings, so we are all-too aware that we may not indulge our wants or appetites. As Lucie said, amongst family and dear friends it is not necessary to be so careful. But out in public, it is a whole other story. Out there, people can be unkind. It is a sad truth of the world, I am afraid."

"I have not had much experience with social constraints." Vivian could not help but feel embarrassed by her faux pas. Had she known what was expected of a lawn party attendee it never would have happened. But she had not, so it had and now all she could do was pick herself up, learn from her mistake and move forward.

It was not as if the world was going to end just because she had behaved like a stable hand.

"Do not fret yourself over it." Lucie sat up straighter and, with a small clap of her hands, turned to Miranda. "We shall take Vivian under our wings. Don't you think it would be an enjoyable venture for all of us? Why, we could brush up on our manners while teaching dear cousin the ins and outs of the rigors of convention. I am sure Mother would approve of our doing so, and there is no harm for any of us in bettering ourselves. You are such a fabulous dancer. I am sure you could teach us some of the latest dances, as well as tutor us in the old stand-bys."

"What fun!" Miranda glowed, her curls bouncing again against her shoulders as she warmed to the idea.

"Vivian? What do you say?"

She met Lucie's gaze. It all sounded a lark, and no one could benefit more from lessons than she.

What do I have to lose? I am here for one grand Season, not to create one embarrassing Season.

"If you do not mind coaching me, I would be extremely grateful for the help." Being anything other than honest was pointless. They already knew she did not know what was expected of her so she could not hide her ignorance. "But I would not feel right if this arrangement is only one-sided. There must be something I can do to repay you."

They shook their heads in unison, but she would not be deterred.

"I insist. You will keep me from making a fool of myself a second time, and I will never be able to thank you for that. And Miranda is going to teach me to dance without trampling all over a gentleman's toes—something every man I partner will never be able to thank her for."

They shared a quiet laugh. Camaraderie had grown between them, and all awkwardness had been banished.

Lucie tapped a finger against her temple. "I am well-read, having devoured nearly all of the books in this very room. You should be able to carry on a conversation with a literary slant, so I shall recommend books which I think may benefit. The first one I think you should read, if you have not already done so, is Miss Jane Austen's *Sense and Sensibility, A Novel by a Lady*. Have you read it?" Vivian shook her head but did not feel self-conscious. Lucie merely nodded, as if she had expected as much. "I shall loan you my copy, and you will begin reading this very day."

"We should begin dance lessons today, as well." Miranda wiggled in her seat, as if she heard musical notes no one else could hear. "The waltz. That is the dance to begin with, I believe."

They had not solved one problem. Vivian might be unschooled, but she had a sense of obligation so she set her heels. "That is all well and good, but we still have not determined what I may do in return. I vow, I will not take part in this endeavor—which, if I may say so, sounds like more fun than I have ever had—unless we can decide upon something that I may do in return. What can I do to repay you?"

"Mother says you are an expert seamstress." Lucie arched one eyebrow. "Is it true?"

Pride had never been one of her sins but now was no time for false modesty. "I am proficient, and have worked on designs sold in London shops. Would you like me to provide dressmaking skills while I am here? I would be only too happy to do so."

"No, you goose. I do not want you to sew for me. I want you to teach me to sew better than I do. I admit, I am all thumbs with a needle, and Miranda is only marginally better than I. Do you think you might help us?"

"I would love to teach you sewing skills. What a wonderful idea."

Miranda had been holding something back. With a glance at Vivian, and then one to Lucie, she said, "Our dear Vivian went riding with Stuart Bailey yesterday. She...ah, she put him in a position where he could not politely refuse her, so when she said she wanted to ride about in his sporty curricle he took her for a spin about the grounds."

"It is good we are getting to our lessons straight away." Lucie did not try to hide her amusement. She laughed openly, the sound bringing matching laughter from the other two. How could anyone not join in when the sound was as inviting as the dainty tinkle of chimes being kissed by a summer breeze?

"I am hopeless, I fear."

"No, you are not hopeless. You have not had the opportunities Miranda and I have had, that is all. We will show people you are a diamond of the first water rather than a woman destined to become an ape leader. Oh yes, cousin, we have some work ahead of us but do not despair. Between us, we shall polish you until your glow positively outshines every other female wishing to make a successful Season for herself. Isn't that right, Miranda?"

"You will win everyone over in no time, Vivian. I am sure of it," Miranda nodded briskly. "*No* time at all!"

She looked from one to the other, wanting to believe them but knowing, in the deepest part of her heart, that she was further from being a London lady than either of them knew.

Work has never scared me before, Vivian thought. Why should it now?

Chapter 6

Oliver had expected Vivian to be surprised by his invitation to accompany him to Town. Frankly, he might have been flabbergasted by the matter as well, had he not been the one making the offer. If he had had more time to consider the options, and weigh her motivations as well as his own, the idea might have seemed less outlandish. But he did not have time to spare; catching a scurrilous thief was a priority.

How could he possibly measure the woman's character and motivations if he did not get to know her better? It was unfeasible. The only solution was to bring her into his company, make her feel comfortable and hope she might divulge something incriminating.

It was unfortunate to suspect Vivian of the break-in at all but the list of suspects was a short one. It was so brief that hers was the only name on the list. He had to find out if she was responsible for the theft, even if it meant squiring her around London.

People will talk, he thought grimly. Let them talk, then! It cannot be helped and if they believe I am keeping company with this distant relation, then let them gossip. At least it will keep every other would-be duchess from fluttering her eyelashes at me.

He was an eligible bachelor. That did not mean he had to like being chased like a rabbit running before a pack of wild dogs. It was not his fault he stood to inherit a title and wealth when his father passed. He would have much rather been someone with less responsibility and more leeway regarding every decision before him—including the choice of a mate.

Many women had tried—unsuccessfully thus far—to court him into a corner but none had seemed more than a passing fancy. They were all so giggly, with their coy smiles and fawning—and feigned, he was certain—interest in anything he said. He could have spoken rubbish and he was sure it would be greeted by a chorus of agreeable nonsense.

They had been riding in silence but Oliver stole a glance at the woman seated beside him. This was the first opportunity to get a close view of her . Every other time they were together there were others about and it hardly seemed mannerly to stare where others would notice.

Vivian Fox was attractive in a way that was so wholly dissimilar to what he was used to seeing that it took a moment to figure out what was different about her beauty. Then, he had it. She took no particular care to enhance the fine features she possessed, unlike the women with whom he regularly came in contact. Her nose, with its slight upturn at the tip, was not dusted with powder. There was no rouge on her rosy pink lips; the dewy shade, so like raspberries after a light rain, was all her own. Nothing enhanced her smooth cheeks; the creamy complexion and sun-kissed cheekbones need no window dressing. And nothing—no cosmetic, trick of the light or artist's palette—could improve upon her stunning violet eyes.

There was no pretense about her. Even the way she sat, with her hands clasped in her lap and her spine arrow-straight, left no room for deception.

How could a woman so completely at home in her own skin be deceitful enough to steal from them? Suddenly the morning's outing seemed a waste of time. There was nothing to learn from her. How could she be hiding anything?

The high-perch phaeton was a particularly dashing vehicle, and their elevated position afforded a stellar view of the passing scenery. He was surprised she had not asked any questions about the sights as they rode by. It occurred to him then that had he been a better host he would have told her about points of interest as they passed them.

"I should have thought to be a more attentive tour guide." He caught the way her eyes grew wide in surprise when he broke the silence. Was she startled by his speaking, or did she have something to hide? It was hard—no, impossible—to tell so he pretended he did not notice the expression. "I keep forgetting this is your first trip to Town. I should be showing you all the points of interest. You must think me completely rag-mannered."

He realized his gaffe the instant the words left his mouth. Of all the stupid things to say.

Vivian's eyes narrowed. Her lips, so inviting and tender-looking just a moment ago, formed a tight line. Then, sarcasm dripping from every word, she said, "I think no such thing. As you well know, I am quite familiar with the manners of the lower classes."

"I did not mean—"

Her gloved had went up like a barrier between them. She did not give him the courtesy of looking at him when she spoke, which made the tiny hairs at the nape of his neck stand straight up. It was an entirely unpleasant sensation, but he could not protest since he had brought her annoyance upon himself.

With a voice chilly enough to drip icicles, "No need to try to explain yourself. I know exactly what you meant."

The effort was futile so he snapped his mouth shut. Why heap more wood on the fire? Her temper already smoldered, so it seemed best to leave her to her own thoughts for a while.

I wish I still took snuff, Oliver thought with a snort of disgust. When he had given up all vices he had included the scented powdered tobacco, something he had wished more than once he had not done. Foolish thing, giving it up. He could use a pinch right about now…a pinch, or mayhap two, to blow the stinging feel of her dressing down right out of his head.

He tugged his top hat to be sure it was angled correctly, and then sat back against the buttery soft leather seat. No expense had been spared when the phaeton had been purchased, so the ride over rutted and cobbled streets was as comfortable as sitting in an armchair beside a blazing hearth.

"Vivian?" Perhaps a safe topic might smooth her ruffled feathers.

To his relief, she did not seem angry when she turned to him. They shared one long seat so when she moved her shoulder brushed his. A whiff of something sweet—lavender, perhaps—filled the air. Now Oliver was grateful his nostrils had not been touched by snuff so he could take full pleasure from the charming scent.

"Yes?" She smiled. It was the teeniest of expressions, but, still, it was something.

"I wondered if you are familiar with the Greek character Phaeton and the myth that surrounds his existence."

Her eyes flashed. She gave him an enormous smile, one that looked almost wide enough to swallow him whole.

Oliver knew how a canary sitting eye-to-eye with a Tabby cat must feel.

In that moment, he realized he had done it again, underestimated her.

He wished he were riding beneath the carriage instead of inside it as he waited for Vivian to speak. Hers was certain to be a scathing retort, one designed to put him firmly in his place and show her superior mind.

If anyone deserved a dressing down, he did. Again.

He almost tumbled from his seat when she smiled sweetly and said, "I confess I am not as well-read in the field of mythology as I would like to be. Greek is particularly unfamiliar to me. It is a situation I hope to remedy in the not-too-distant future but for now I am, to my chagrin, not entirely certain who Phaeton was. Do you mind giving a lesson?"

He thought it a trick designed to lull him into a false sense of superiority. So Miss Fox was not as dissimilar to London ladies as she would have him believe.

"Of course." They were nearing the turn to the Tattersall Market so the conversation would have to be very brief. "Phaeton was a character in Greek mythology, and is, as I am sure you must have surmised by now, the one after whom a conveyance such as we are riding in is named. Phaeton is remembered most vividly for what might be called an unfortunate decision."

"How so?"

"Well, he attempted to drive his father's chariot into the sun. The ensuing chaos nearly destroyed the world."

The way her eyebrows shot up at his explanation showed clear surprise. If she was pretending to know less than she did, she was a stellar actress.

Perhaps a career on the stage would suit, Oliver thought. Although…could it be that she is not playacting?

"Not a very good way to leave one's mark on history," Vivian said.

"No, it isn't. While Phaeton is remembered, it is not with fondness."

"I should say not!"

The phaeton turned into Tattersall's drive, joining several others in a queue toward the market's front entrance. Apparently he was not the only one with a mind to purchasing horses on the warm day.

The sweet scent of hay reached them as they inched closer to the place where they would leave the carriage and proceed on foot.

Oliver heard his companion gasp, and when he turned and saw what she had spied he knew why she reacted thusly. A lovely gray mare was being led about by a stable hand in the grassy area adjacent to the marketplace. The animal was easily sixteen hands high but looked gentle enough for a child to ride. With its head held high, mane dancing in the slight breeze pushed up by the passing carriages, the horse did not seem at all put out by the attention she drew.

"Oh…isn't she beautiful?" Her words came in a

whisper but the feeling from her heart was so forceful that he did not need to lean close to hear her.

He dropped his gaze from the horse to his guest, and thought that she was by far the prettiest sight he had witnessed in a long time.

Silently shaking himself, Oliver pulled his opinions onto a more suitable area. Horses. He was here to purchase spare horses for the upcoming fox hunt. That was the only thing that need concern him. Horses, and the manor thief.

Still, she deserved a reply so he swallowed hard. He had not expected her presence to affect him in any way other than by giving credence to his suspicions. Now that they had ridden and chatted, he was less confident than before that he had the right person under his eye.

He admonished himself not to be fooled by a woman's charm. Thieves earned their way in the world by being deceitful.

"Do you see her? Isn't she magnificent?" Vivian placed a hand on his wrist and gave it a gentle squeeze. Her excitement sent a thrill to his core, almost as if she had infused some of her energy into his flesh.

"I do." Her delight brought a chuckle, and he was glad he had asked her along. Even if she did turn out to be a thief, the outing was proving to be a pleasurable one. "And she is magnificent. You have a keen eye for horses. A very keen eye."

****

Vivian could not wait for the carriage—the phaeton, as her annoying host had made the point—to arrive at their destination. She could have gladly dropped Oliver off at the front door and instructed the driver to keep on going. Where? It hardly mattered, as long as it was miles from the insufferable man who sat stonily by her side.

The day had begun on such a high note.

I should have known better than to fall for his ruse, she thought. A spark of anger in response to having been lulled into a false sense of camaraderie with the man, sent heat spiraling through her. How could she have been so stupid? He cared for no one save himself.

She took a deep, steadying breath. They had just turned in the entrance to the estate. The long, winding cobbled stone lane would take a while to cover. Perhaps there was some way for them to find middle ground yet.

Vivian counted to ten. Then, she counted ten more. When she was sufficiently certain she would not lose her temper again she turned slightly on the bench seat and faced Oliver.

He looked as unperturbed by their recent disagreement as if it had never taken place. Their harsh words and twin fits of temper seemed not to have disturbed his day one whit.

Oliver's complacency annoyed Vivian once more. Inhaling, and holding the breath, she gave the ten-count a third attempt.

She had never been called stubborn to her face but she knew she had an obstinate streak as wide as the lane they now travelled down her spine. It was, her mother was never shy to remind her, an unladylike trait. Furthermore, it was not an attractive attribute, to posses such a headstrong personality. Vivian endeavored to better herself at all opportunities, as her recent arrangement with Lucie and Miranda surely underscored. The obdurate streak, however, was almost impossible to control.

How could he be so pig-headed?

Again her mother's words filled her mind, and she was reminded that bees were more attracted to honey than vinegar so she pasted a smile on her face. Idly she wondered if donkeys or swine favored honey, as well, but she rapidly squashed the idea. It would not do to laugh in the man's face, even if he did not seem to be bothered by their disagreement.

It did not make sense to care so much about his feelings when it was apparent he did not give a fig about hers.

Still…

The bee. Honey. Vinegar. All right, she had it. She thought. Perhaps.

"I do believe we started this excursion on the right foot. And, I must add, I appreciate your inviting me along. As I said, I think we began the day brilliantly." She waited for his reply but one did not come. A gentle push, then, toward reconciliation. "Oliver? Don't you think we got off to a good start?"

In a voice designed, she was sure, to calm rather than provoke, he said, "We did, at that. I am…" Inhaling as deeply as she had just a moment before, he paused. Then, "I am pleased you accepted my invitation. I hope it was received in the manner it was intended. That is, I trust you wished to get to know me better. For my part, I wanted us to become more closely acquainted. We are, as you well know, destined to be thrown together at parties, sporting events and other social engagements all Season long."

"Moreover, we live in the same house," Vivian pointed out with a smile. They were getting somewhere.

Perhaps he was not as calloused as his earlier behavior indicated. A softer core to the hardened exterior?

"Good point. I suppose we will be seeing an awful lot of each other for the next few months."

She had never been one to use feminine wiles to turn a man's head. There had never been any heads to turn, since she was by far too busy working and caring for Liam to have time for suitors. Besides, Vivian was not at all certain she *had* any wiles to employ.

But now that she was as a foreigner in a strange land she had to use every tool at her disposal. With that in mind, she gave a tiny laugh and said, "Oh, I hope the months won't be too awful."

Her joke did not pass without comment. Chuckling, Oliver added, "As do I."

They shared a quiet moment, the horses' hooves the only accompaniment to their private musings. Then, feeling like she had gained some ground with him, she pressed forward.

"Our splendid beginning gave way to a less-than-ideal ending, didn't it?"

A sigh. He spread his hands wide, palms toward the canopy of drooping elm limbs hanging above them. "I am afraid it did. It was not the way I planned our excursion to turn out. I had thought to take you for a persimmon ice at the sweet shop but by the time we left Tattersall's I knew you were in no mood for it so I did not ask."

Sadness pierced her heart. So many opportunities had been out of her reach that to miss even one brought a smattering of melancholy.

"I would have liked persimmon ice, I think." It was the truth, even though she was not completely sure she knew exactly what a persimmon ice consisted of. Still, it sounded wonderful.

Oliver straightened, and reached an arm out toward the driver's back. "I do not wish to deprive you of the pleasure, especially if it brings you one minute of sorrow to miss the treat. Would you like me to tell Bradshaw to turn around? We can go back, and I will gladly purchase all the persimmon ices you care to consume. Would you like that?"

She was touched by his solicitude. Impulsively she leaned over and put her hand on his arm, stilling him. Oliver's jacket was sun-warmed, and her palm felt instantly hotter. It was not a searing heat, and would have felt comfortable had they not been arguing almost the entire way home. Still, the hope of peace hovered over them, so she ran her hand down his arm and boldly took his hand.

Neither Lucie nor Miranda would call this proper, but they are not here to see. Besides, if I have to use an extra bit of honey to have him see reason, so be it.

Oliver's gaze dropped to their linked hands. He held hers loosely at first, then more boldly after she gave his fingers a tiny squeeze.

"I am overwhelmed by your kindness. It is lovely of you to offer to turn the carriage around but I do not think now is the proper time. We may be missed if we are gone too long, and I do not wish to worry your mother."

A slanted grin made him look slightly roguish. "Mother will not worry overmuch. She has high hopes of you and I...well, let us just say my mother is hoping—as I think yours must be, as well—that you and I find pleasure in each other's company. I believe

Mother would see our tarrying as a good sign."

How could she have been so naïve? Of course their mothers hoped they would get along. Marrying Oliver would be the answer to any mother's matrimonial dreams. She supposed there must be something about her, be it her character or the feelings of indebtedness felt toward her mother, which made her a suitable candidate for Oliver's attention.

With a burst of clarity came a loss for words. Vivian could not think of anything to say, nothing to do and, trapped as she was in the carriage, nowhere to go to escape the reality of her situation. She tugged her hand, but the fingers threaded through hers tightened.

She saw what he meant to do a scant second before he did it. Feeling like a mouse caught in a trap, she did not even turn her head away. There was no time, and it would have done her no good anyhow. If there was one thing she had learned during her short association with Oliver Gregory, it was that he did not tolerate failure. He got what he wanted, when he desired it and by whatever means necessary to achieve success. His behavior at Tattersall's had illustrated that clearly.

The touch of his lips on hers was subtle, as if neither knew where the moment should take them. Then, he pressed his mouth firmly against hers. The feel of his lips was pleasant but did not inspire any warm emotions within her. There were no sparks, no trembling hands or fluttering heartbeats. While his kiss was nice, it was not captivating.

When the kiss ended, she saw her feelings reflected in his eyes.

Whatever their mothers might want, theirs was not a match destined for romantic history. Vivian knew it, and she saw Oliver did, as well.

Releasing her hand, and inquiring as politely as if he had not just stolen a kiss, Oliver cleared his throat. "So we shall indulge ourselves at another time, then? Persimmon ices will taste just as refreshing later in the week. Shall we plan on getting some then, and heading home now? Would that suit you?"

"It would suit me perfectly."

Regardless of what their mothers wanted, Vivian did not see how she and Oliver could ever be more than just friends. And, if today's difference of opinion meant anything, she was not even certain they could maintain any kind of friendship. After all, friends needed to at least like each other, and liking the man who had just stolen a kiss was the furthest thing from her mind as the carriage rolled to a stop before the manor's front door.

****

Vivian's skirt switched alluringly as she dashed up the front stairs. Oliver watched, thinking she looked as if a bevy of ghouls were on her tail.

Was he so gruesome that he inspired such fleet-footedness? Surely he could not be that distasteful. She had seemed to enjoy herself at Tattersall's—so much so he had decided to invite her to accompany him on his next jaunt to the horse market.

But that was before their unfortunate squabbling had begun. She had seemed so level-headed, with a keen intelligence and candid observations. How had it happened that she was witty and fun one moment and unreasonable, inflexible, opinionated and a wealth of other equally unflattering characteristics the next? Vivian was like one of those pinwheels made of double-sided paper. When the breeze blew, one pattern turned to the next. Then, when the wind blew a second time, the pattern reversed. They had made him dizzy when he was a little boy. Now, dealing with a woman who reminded him of a child's toy made his childhood dizziness look like nothing.

How to figure a woman out, especially one unlike any he had met before? It seemed utterly beyond his reach.

He followed her inside, handed his gloves to the servant beside the door and would have gone directly upstairs had his arrival not been discovered.

"Darling, is that you?" His mother's sweet voice could not be ignored, so he headed down the wide hallway toward her private sitting room. He found her as he thought he would, with her embroidery hoop in her hand and a length of colored floss trailing from her needle. She looked up and placed the needlework on her lap when he walked in. "Oliver? Is something wrong?"

Dropping none-too-gently into a heavily upholstered chair designed, he was certain, for a body much more compact than his tall, muscular frame, he slapped a hand against his thigh. A tiny cloud of dust rose, remnant of the ride in the open carriage. "What do you mean? Why should anything be wrong?"

He should have known better than to try to fool her. She cast a look that needed no words. Then she crossed her hands, the same way he guessed her ankles were crossed beneath het skirts, and waited.

Mothers and tax collectors had one thing in common: One could only avoid dealing directly with them for just so long. Then, the piper got his due.

With a sigh, Oliver shrugged. Whatever

speculation she had was probably fairly close to the truth. There was no need to keep her in suspense, so he did not try to do so.

He chuckled. "I shall tell you what you want to know if you tell me how you knew anything was amiss. Even before you saw me, you knew something was not quite right, didn't you?"

"Of course I did. And it was an easy deduction, too."

"How?"

Lady Gregory shook her head, as if the explanation was obvious. "I heard Vivian fly up the stairs. It can only mean one thing. Either you have angered her, or you have insulted her. Which was it?"

"Both," he admitted.

"Oh, Oliver, you didn't. Vivian is a guest in this house—you simply cannot annoy and insult the guests. It has never been done before and I will not have you setting a precedence."

He wished he knew how to undo the events of the latter half of the morning, wanted to take back most of what he had said and almost all of what he had done—including the humdrum kiss—but he could not. What was done was done, and there was no retracting his words or behavior. Miss Fox would just have to deal with it—all of it.

"I am afraid it is too late, Mother." He made a regretful noise deep in his throat and scrubbed his hands through his hair. "I have already done both, and there is nothing that can be done to erase that fact."

She pulled her eyebrows together, looking uncharacteristically cross with him.

"Stop that—you already look like a porcupine and

mussing your hair again is only going to make it worse. That is not a good habit, pulling your curls askew every time your mind is challenged. Why, it is no wonder you insulted poor Vivian, with a hair style like that. It is a miracle you did not scare the poor girl to death."

Poor *Vivian*?

"I will stop but I promise you, your 'poor Vivian' is much more porcupine-y than I ever will be. She is…she has…oh, and her temper. Why, that is—oh, dash it all! Why are we discussing her anyway? Don't we have something more agreeable to talk about?"

Women were supposed to be a joyful addition to a man's life, not a thorn in his side. How did he get so involved with such a difficult female?

Then, he relented. "Oh…she is not all that bad-tempered. Not really."

"Bad-tempered? Vivian? Surely you cannot mean that." The scandalized expression on his mother's face was as readable as any of the volumes in the family library. She was wondering if he was beginning to lose his mind again; he saw it in her eyes and in the set of her mouth. Then, he heard it in her voice. "Oliver? Are you sure you are seeing things as they truly are? Are you sure you are not imagining Vivian is someone else?"

"I am not imagining anything. There is no need to worry. I am not going daft and will definitely not need a room at Bedlam—not this week, anyhow." The joke fell flat, so he went on. "We had a quarrel, that is all. It was actually a minor row, now that I think back. She fell in love with one of the horses I bought for the fox hunt. That was fine but she went on and on about how wonderful it must be to be able to place such a beautiful animal in such a fabulous setting, with a roomy stall and all it will be able to eat…you get the idea."

His mother removed the embroidery hoop from her lap and placed it on the low mahogany table beside her chair. "It sounds like you had a perfectly ordinary conversation. Where is the quarrel in an exchange like that?"

Had he withheld information there would not have been a quarrel but he had not known his being forthright would send her into such a tizzy.

"We only fell out when I told her the animal would probably be sold after the hunt." He wished he had not told her. "I tried to explain that I bought today's horses as spares, in the event someone came up without a mount. She did not see my point of view—not at all—and insisted I am heartless."

"Oh, my dear, you know you are not heartless," Lady Gregory said softly. A mother's gaze made the statement a caress. "She is not used to horses being stabled in private homes. Why, Vivian is thinking the horse will become a family pet."

"Exactly." His shoulders were heavy and a sudden tiredness swept over him. The weight of the estate, its inhabitants and entertainments, as well as his personal feelings of unrest made the very air seem denser, harder to breathe.

"You tried to explain?"

He nodded. "I did."

"She could not see your side of the transaction?"

His fingers itched with the desire to plow through his hair again but he grasped the arms of the chair and held on tightly. "She could not. No matter what I said, she would not be swayed. I angered her with my—how did she put it? Oh, right…she called me cold-blooded, that was it."

An amused snort, so unladylike yet so fitting, came from his mother. Oliver's load lightened, her understanding making his burdens seem much less strenuous. He chuckled, shaking his head.

It was almost beyond belief that an outing designed to discover thievery could end so badly.

"So, you annoyed her with your callous indifference to the fate of the horse. You said you annoyed and insulted her. I am almost afraid to inquire, but how did you insult Vivian?"

It was Oliver's turn to snort, and he did so with more gusto than his mother had.

"I kissed her."

Chapter 7

The only reasonable explanation Vivian could fathom for Jenny bringing her breakfast tray in the wee morning hours, long before she typically rose, was through some kind of below-stairs telepathy. There was no other rationalization for the maid's providing that which its recipient did not yet desire.

Jenny had long since collected the breakfast tray. And while she had not known she was hungry before its arrival, Vivian managed to polish off every bite of each delectable morsel. The wide array of food and in such copious quantities quite turned her head, as well as filled her stomach. This morning there had been blueberry scones, cinnamon toast and a pineapple-and-lemon puree which literally melted on her tongue.

She was sure to gain weight eating so well but she did not care. Her figure was much less shapely than was currently the fashion so a bit of extra padding could only be in her favor.

No matter how hard she tried, this morning she simply could not become interested in anything, not even the novel she had been practically inhaling since Lucie loaned it to her. It was futile to pretend to care about practical Elinor's yearning for a man promised to another. She was equally indifferent to Marianne's sentimental romantic journey. It had nothing whatsoever to do with Miss Austen's flair for storytelling. Thus far Vivian had loved every passage in *Sense and Sensibility* and would, no doubt, continue to be enchanted through to the very last word—another time.

Even with her belly full and soft murmurings of the household coming awake, she simply could not concentrate. Try as she might, there seemed nothing capable of holding her attention for more than a fleeting moment or two.

She paced the room like a caged animal.

I cannot walk circles about the room. I shall wear the floorboards out.

Taking one last turn around the space, she weighed her options. It was mid-morning, but there was still an air of just waking in the hurried footsteps and hushed snippets of conversation that passed in the hallway. It would not do to engage in a noisy endeavor—not that she was overly skilled at any of the loudest of ladylike hobbies. Vivian did not play the pianoforte, having never been given the opportunity to learn, but she considered it the loudest leisure pursuit. A walk in the gardens might be nice, especially with the sun far from its zenith, but interrupting the groundskeepers in their early pruning and clipping duties seemed somewhat forward. What if there was some unwritten rule that denied guests from meandering before, say, noon? How would it look if she appeared suddenly amongst the roses like an unwelcome insect?

Neither strolling nor exercising her non-existent musical talents seemed the proper way to pass the time.

The only thing she knew how to do well was sew. Even thought she had come to the manor hoping to broaden her horizons, she was still woefully inadequate at any genteel art that did not involve holding a needle above fabric.

Sitting heavily on the cushioned window seat, Vivian lifted an embroidery hoop holding a large square of Irish linen tautly in its grip. A length of lilac floss dangled from the fabric. She threaded the floss through the tiny eye of her needle and surveyed the project with a critical eye.

It had been ages since she had worked a sampler. Her hands were ordinarily occupied with stitching to produce an income that this simply-for-pleasure endeavor was a real treat.

The sampler was still more in her head than on the fabric, but she could already see her vision coming to life. A ribbon of ivy leaves wound down the left side, and would anchor the profusion of flowers she planned to embroider in the remaining space. One of Lady Gregory's flower gardens was her inspiration. Located near the greenhouse a short distance from an orderly row of crimson rosebushes, the wildflower garden was a riot of colors and textures. Naturally, it smelled heavenly but that could not be captured by her needle and thread.

The soothing rhythm of pushing thread through the fabric and smoothing the stitches into place was calming. Her breathing slowed and her heart stopped beating in her chest like a trapped bird hammering against a window pane. The tightness in her throat eased and the turmoil of the past days slid from her mind.

Time passed swiftly. Palest pink peonies, ruffled yellow-and-red tulips and lavender wisteria bloomed on the linen. She worked quickly and efficiently, her fingers moving almost without any conscious direction.

Relaxation brought an ease in decorum. Vivian's slippers had been kicked off and her feet tucked beneath her almost as soon as she began embroidering. The window seat, with its long, wide cushion cradled in a deep nook, was the ideal spot for letting her guard down. She had pushed up the window casing at the far end of the window seat, and a gentle draft caressed her face and hands.

She was so content, and so entirely caught up in her embroidery, that she almost did not hear the call. It was faint, borne on the slow breeze. Had the room not been so still she surely would have missed it.

"Help…"

She stilled her needle, wondering if she had imagined the cry.

Then, it came again. The sound was weak, but it was real.

"Help…"

Vivian stuck her needle in the edge of the linen so it would not get lost. She pushed the floss and scissors aside, dropped the embroidery hoop over the smaller accoutrements and tilted her head toward the open window. Patience did not come easily but she waited, slipping her feet into her slippers as she did so.

Finally, she heard the cry again. It seemed to be coming from nearby—but where?

She crossed the room, opened the door and stuck her head into the corridor. It was empty and this far from the open window she could not even hear the elm leaves in the big tree outside her window rustling together. Vivian waited, tapping her toe against the wool carpet runner.

When the plea came, it was a trifle louder and came from the far end of the corridor. She hurried down the hallway, stopping every few steps to listen in case the call came again. It did not. She made it all the way to the end of the hallway, to a junction with two stairwells. One led down, the other went up.

I am truly at a crossroad. She pulled her lower lip between her teeth, gazing at both sets of stairs.

The cry sounded still louder when it came once again. There could be no mistake; whoever was calling for help was upstairs.

Gathering her skirt in her hand and hiking the hem up high, she began climbing the steep stairs. They were not like any of the other staircases she had traveled in the manor. After the short ascent to a landing, these steps grew narrow and led upward at an almost dangerous incline. A cobweb dangled a corner above her head as she passed beneath it. There was a general air of disuse about the flight of steps.

By the time she reached the last step she was winded, so she paused for a moment to get her bearings. The staircase left off in a hallway. It was not as grand or as wide as the one below, but there were doors lining it in a similar fashion to the floor where her room was.

The dusty air was silent. Where could the call for help come from? There did not seem to be anyone about, yet she was sure the noise had come from somewhere up here.

A bead of perspiration slid down her neck and into the back of her dress. If she did not hurry she would, no doubt, be entirely wilted. The temperature was near scorching, and without any current the place felt like the inside of a bread oven.

She did not want to venture further, and would have loved to seek the comfort of her cozy window seat, but it did not seem right to simply turn around and leave. Suppose someone was in desperate need, and she disregarded the fact in favor of her own ease? She had not been raised to be selfish, and could not begin to favor the trait now.

Vivian proceeded slowly down the hallway, opening each closed door she passed and peeking in. Most of the rooms were filled with sheet-shrouded furnishings, and looked like they had not had a footstep cross their floors in years. Every time she checked a room and found it lacking a human presence, she closed its door firmly behind her. Before long, she had checked more than half the rooms and had found no one in need of assistance.

Pushing a fallen lock of hair off her cheek with a grimy hand, Vivian paused at the end of the hallway. She had checked the rooms on one side; there were only a dozen or so rooms left to check and still there was no sign of life.

What if she had imagined the cry for help?

Worse yet, what if the call had not been human?

Vivian chased the ghostly thought from her mind. She did not believe in the supernatural, preferring to give credence to only that which she could explain in a logical manner.

Ghosts? The whole idea is preposterous!

"Help me. Please, won't someone help me?"

Thoughts scattered as Vivian followed the sound. One door was ever-so slightly ajar, so she pushed it open and dashed into the room. It too was filled with covered furniture but near a huge fireplace there were three black-bristled brushes. A black footprint marked the floor beside the tools.

She crossed the room. She stood beside the fireplace, wondering how to proceed, when the voice called again.

"Help—please, help me!"

She bent, and then took a deep breath as she ducked into the empty fireplace opening. It was only about waist-high so she had to nearly double over to fit inside the space. A larger person would have been denied access to the spot, or might have found themselves stuck had the thought to push into the fireplace struck them. She could not imagine why anyone would want to do so.

Soot fell in clumps on her head and shoulders as she lifted her face to peer into the chimney. The view was not what she expected it to be. Where light from the sun should have been, there was only darkness. Then, as her eyes adjusted to the gloom, she saw the darkness shift.

"Hello?" She spoke in a normal tone of voice but in the confined space it sounded loud, even to her own ears.

Closing her eyes as the shape above her sent a fresh shower of creosote and cinders down on her, Vivian asked the obvious in a gentle tone. "Are you stuck?"

The voice belonged to a child. "I am, Your Ladyship."

Vivian swallowed her laughter, not wishing to offend the young man who, even in his dire position, remembered his manners.

"'Miss' will do for now."

She wondered how best to extricate the fellow. His legs straddled the rectangular opening, and his boots were planted on two opposing walls just above her head.

"We shall have you out of here shortly," she said, pretending confidence she did not possess.

Liam had gotten into all sorts of tight spots and she had always managed to pull him out but he had never wedged himself as firmly into a chimney as this child had. It would not do to hurt him by yanking him down but she could not leave him like a cork in a bottle forever.

"How exactly did you get yourself in there? And what, precisely, is stuck?" Logic told her to proceed in reverse order, simply undoing whatever he had unwittingly done.

"I climbed in, miss. And it's my shoulders. I thought I could brush up another level or two but when I reached high my arm twisted. When that happened, my shoulders went sideways and I—"

She hated to cut him off but it was getting hotter by the minute in the tight space. Long explanations were fine in their place, but this was definitely not the place.

"I get the idea." She placed her hands around his ankles. "Can you let yourself dangle?"

"What if I fall? I could break my bloody head!"

Vivian stifled a laugh. "I promise I won't let you fall and break your...well, I won't let you fall, that's all. I am right below you so I am in a grand position to catch you when you come loose. Trust me, won't you? I have a younger brother and I am always rescuing him."

He sounded unsure. "You do? Have a brother, that is?"

Sweat rolled down her spine. Sticky from the heat and filthy from the soot, she was in need of soap and water but that would have to wait. First, she had to convince her new friend to trust her. It seemed he was not the trusting type.

"I do. His name is Liam." She wiped the side of her face with her shoulder. "I have never dropped him, and I will not drop you. Now, the only way I can see to get you out of here—and me, as well—is to pull you out. You will drop into my arms and we shall both leave this stuffy chimney behind. Sound like something you might care to try?"

When his response did not immediately come, Vivian considered—then discarded—the thought that pulling him without his consent might be the best way to proceed. She was sure she could have done it but doing so would not instill trust in this little fellow, so she waited.

"All right, miss. If you're sure…"

"I am. Now, let go of the walls with your feet. Just let them hang…" The burnt taste of soot filled her mouth as it fell off the soles of his boots. "That's right. I am going to pull you, ever-so-gently so don't be frightened—"

Vivian tugged his legs hard, knowing in her heart that he was not going to come free unless she took drastic action. Relief coursed through her when she felt him slip from the chimney and onto her. They both tumbled to the hearth in a tangle of arms and legs. A chimney brush plopped onto the center of the skirt of her borrowed lavender dress.

The child in her lap could not have been more than five or six. His smile, so bright against his filthy face, made her forget her wardrobe woes.

"You unstuck me! Thank you, miss! It feels ever so much better not to be up there."

"You're very welcome." She ran her hands lightly over his shoulders and arms, and through his hair. "Are you broken anywhere?"

"Nah, I didn't hurt myself. I did make a mess of you, though." He brushed a cinder off her right sleeve, leaving a black trail behind. "Oh, miss! I am sorry!"

"Don't fret. I am sure this can be laundered out." She knew the stains would never come clean but smiled anyway. "Now, what do you say we climb out of here? It is too hot by far to sit here and chat all day."

The child scrambled off her lap and crawled from the fireplace. She gathered her ruined skirt around her knees and did the same. When a hand suddenly came into view in front of her face, Vivian stopped moving and craned her neck backward.

"May I be of service?" Will Fulbright's hand looked much too fresh to touch but there was no polite way to refuse it. She put her dirty hand in his unsoiled one and allowed him to help her to her feet. "Are you all right?"

He held her hand longer than was absolutely necessary. Heat warmed her cheeks. This time her sheen had nothing to do with the fireplace or its chimney. Will's thumb traced a lazy circle on her palm, sending a thrill straight to her heart.

Brushing her free hand down the front of her skirt did nothing whatsoever to improve her appearance. A smudge, no doubt from the grit on her palm, appeared on the fine fabric.

Botheration! I shall have to repay Lucie for this

dress—somehow.

"I am fine," Vivian said with a small nod. She smiled when Will clutched her hand tightly before releasing it. His concern showed clearly in his expression, so she rushed to reassure him. "Truly, Mr. Fulbright, I am just fine."

"I am relieved to hear that." Then he turned to the small boy by his side. "And what about you, chap? Are you unhurt after your unlucky journey into the chimney?"

"No harm done, Your Lordship." A smart tug on the brim of the blackened cap he wore sent a cloud of soot falling around the child's slight frame.

"Glad to hear it. And you may call me 'sir'. I am not anyone's lordship." Will gave the boy's cap brim a teasing pull, and asked, "And what is your name? I do trust you have one—and I shall bet it is a jolly good name, as well. So? Care to tell us who you are?"

The easy banter between man and boy captivated Vivian. She could not help but wish that Liam had the type of male companionship the two before her fell so conveniently into. They seemed to take it as their due, the friendship that bloomed over a tug or two on a hat and a brief introduction.

Poor Liam. He has missed so much, and does not even know it.

"My name is Edward but no one calls me that except my Gram."

"What does everyone else call you, then?" The boy's mischievous grin did not fit the staid name. Vivian could not picture him being called "Ed" either, so when he chortled his answer she was not surprised.

"Why, everyone calls me Eddie, sir! My mum says

that she should've called me that from the first, and not have bothered with anything proper." He removed his cap and smacked it against his thigh. A fresh wave of dust rose in the air but it did not matter. Both Vivian and the boy were filthy, and if Mr. Fulbright lingered much longer he would surely end up dirty as well. Slapping his hat back onto his head, the child shrugged. "All I know is I've got an easy name to hear. When Mum hollers for me, I know it's me she wants. Not a lot of Eddies, you know. Loads of Johns and Jacks but not so many Eddies. That's all that really matters, Mum says."

Vivian had missed something. "What's all that matters?"

As philosophically as a young child might, he shrugged and said, "Why, knowing where your home is, miss. Mum says that as long as I know where to go when I'm called, I'll always be all right. She says the heart'll lead me home every time. That's what she says, leastways."

"Your mother is a smart woman." It was hard, but she kept her voice from giving any hint at the lump that had formed in her throat.

"I think so. Well, thanks a bunch for pulling me out of the chimney, miss." Eddie tipped his cap. Then he turned to the man and said, "And thank you, sir, for helping get us both out of there." He gathered his brushes, tucked them beneath one arm and turned for the door. Pausing in the doorway, he looked seriously at Vivian. "Now don't you go getting ideas about climbing in there again, miss. It's no place for a lady."

"I shall remember that, Eddie. Thank you for the advice." Vivian dipped a tiny curtsey as Eddie dashed out the door and down the hallway. They heard his footsteps grow faint. Then, the sound of his boot soles on the stairs.

When they were alone, she became conscious of her dishevelment. She did not know why it mattered, only that it did.

As if reading her mind, Mr. Fulbright reached out and swept a fingertip over her cheek. To her horror, when he pulled it back it was blackened.

"Oh, I know I look awful. I did not plan…that is, I do not make it a habit of—"

"Rescuing small boys? Really, Miss Fox, do not apologize. Who knows how long that climbing boy would have been trapped in the chimney if you had not come to his aid?" His smile was warm, and his words equally so.

Vivian forgot her appearance when his gaze caught hers. The flecks of amber in the man's eyes looked like bits of gold, and she could not pull her gaze from his.

A woman could get lost in those eyes.

When Mr. Fulbright placed a hand on her shoulder and leaned close, his eyebrows knit, she realized she was staring. Mortification made her face hotter, and she dropped her gaze to the floorboards as she scrambled for some way to extricate herself.

"Are you sure you are all right?"

She nodded. "I am fine, thank you." Then a thought struck her. She looked up and asked, "How did you know the climbing boy was missing?"

He put his hand in his trouser pocket and rocked back on his heels. "I met the chimney sweep as he was coming down from the roof. He asked if I had seen a young boy. When I said I had not, he said the climbing boy had gone into one of the chimneys over an hour before. I just assumed he was stuck somewhere, so I came to take a look."

"How did you know exactly which floor he was on? More to the point—how did you decide which room to search?"

The manor had several chimneys, and numerous fireplaces. It seemed a miracle that the boy had been found at all.

"Why, I followed your trail, of course." Mr. Fulbright grinned, looking so satisfied that she smiled in return.

"My trail?"

When he pulled his hand from his pocket and uncurled his fist, two lengths of lavender embroidery floss laid across his palm. "Your trail, Miss Fox. One on the stairs and the other was just outside the door. So, you see, it was not at all difficult to track you—and Eddie—down. Quite easy, in fact."

****

"So you are saying you did not have a pleasant excursion with Vivian? Is that it?"

Oliver hated to displease his mother but he could not give her what she so plainly sought. Still, it would not do to make the outing sound as if it had been to the devil's lair instead of the horse auction.

"I thought we discussed this yesterday when I returned home." Had he realized he would be rehashing yesterday's news, he would have remained in his rooms.

"Yesterday you were less than chatty. I know you well; there are things you are not telling me about what went on in Town. Standing in for Vivian's mother, as I am while she is visiting, gives me cause to understand what—and who—may be vexing the poor girl." His mother watched him over the rim of her tea cup. "So, you are saying you did not have a pleasant time with her?"

"I am saying that our trip to Tattersall's was not as enjoyable as I had hoped it would be." He stood, and then proceeded to pace the floor in his mother's sitting room. There were numerous hassocks and tables filled with bric-a-brac to avoid so his stride was shorter than the norm but just being up and about released some of the pent-up energy that pulsed through him. Oliver took a full turn around the room before he spoke again. "Actually, the ride there, as well as most of the hours we spent at the auction, was agreeable. It wasn't until I purchased a lovely gray mare that Vivian cut up my peace."

"What disturbed her? The horse could not have been a bone-setter, not if it was up for sale at the auction." Lady Gregory frowned, a gesture Oliver saw so infrequently it held his attention for almost a full minute. He stared at her until she prompted, "Well? Oliver? Are you listening to me, or am I just sitting here talking to myself?"

"I am sorry. I am listening—and you are not talking to yourself, I promise."

"That is good to hear. Talking to oneself, especially at my age, is not advantageous. It might get me a padded room at Bedlam if anyone caught me at it." Her eyes sparkled, the frown on her face pulled up to a twitching smile.

The joke hit its mark. He stopped pacing, sat down in the chair across from hers and chuckled. Shaking his head, Oliver said, "Oh, Mother, you are a lark. No one would ever take you for being befogged. Quite the opposite, in fact. You are the one person I know who always seems to put a finger on the pulse of a situation."

"Tell me the situation, then, and we will see if we can unravel what has you so tied up," Lady Gregory said gently.

When he was a little boy he had sat in this very same room and heard those exact words on many occasions. Then, his troubles had been of the quickly solvable, boyish variety. Now, they were more complicated and while he loved his mother's willingness to help he was not at all sure she could "unravel" things that easily.

What did he have to lose? He was getting no closer to tracking down the thief or discerning the intricacies of their visitor's character than he had been a day ago. Why not get another perspective?

"Vivian seemed to get pleasure from looking at the horses. She petted many but fell in love with the one gray mare. I thought she would be happy when it was one of those I purchased."

He paused, the recollection of her joyful laughter at the moment she realized the gray was his causing his heart to swell. She had clapped her hands the way an entertained child might, and he had loved seeing her so pleased.

Then, things had turned unpleasant.

Oliver shook his head but he could not erase the memory of the harsh words they had shared. "She got annoyed when she found out that most, if not all, of the horses I bought yesterday will be sold once the fox hunt is over. She does not care for the idea at all, and says that it is a... She said that I am..." He still could not believe what she had said, what she had accused him of being. No one—not even when he was at his most pitiful or furthest out of control—had called him what she had. No one!

"What did she say, dear? It cannot have been that bad."

His mouth tasted sour, as if he had swallowed a cupful of vinegar. "She said that it is cruel to sell the horses just when they will grow accustomed to living here. And she said that I am..."

"What did she call you?"

He swallowed the sour taste in his mouth, and then spat the word. "Heartless. She says only someone without any heart would do something so cruel."

Lady Gregory sat back in her chair and crossed her legs. One foot wiggled in midair, sending the hemline of her skirt fluttering. She looked dangerously close to laughing, although he could not see how she could feel thusly. How could she be amused by his dressing down?

"You said as much yesterday. Now, dear, you cannot believe she actually meant that. It is evident that you two were on opposing sides of the fence, that's all. Why, Vivian would think that the horses should remain at in our stables. Why would she feel they should be shuffled off to other estates when they might have a comfortable existence right here?"

She had a point, but he did not feel like giving in. Oliver sniffed his disagreement, which brought a fresh glance of amusement his way.

"I thought you would be on my side."

"I am not on anyone's side." Her tone was soft by comparison to his rough one. "I am only pointing out that Vivian would think anyone heartless who would turn any creature out."

"It is not as if I plan on setting them loose on London's streets, left alone to fend for themselves. I would find them fine homes, the way Father did when he thinned out the stables. This is no different—why, Father has been furnishing mounts for guests for years, and has always resold the horses once they have provided service. It is nothing new."

She tapped a finger against the side of her nose. Today she wore a dress of the softest green silk, and looked years younger than her actual age. The girlish nose-tapping gesture gave her the appearance of being even more youthful.

"Not to you or me. We are used to the ins and outs of fox hunts and other social events. But our guest is not, remember? To her, selling the horses is like letting go of family pets—unthinkable, cruel and heartless. Don't you see? She does not object to you, Oliver. She just does not understand the common practices we take for granted."

He mulled his mother's words over for a long, silent moment. She did make some good points, and seeing the situation through her eyes did give it a different slant.

Still, he could not believe all Vivian's objections had been over the horses.

"I don't agree with everything you say. I think— from the bottom of my heartless soul—that our dear houseguest does not like me one bit. She and I are like oil and water—incompatible and complete opposites. I am sorry, but it is the truth."

"Are you certain?"

"I know you want it to be different, but Miss Fox and I are just not suited for each other. Why, we cannot even take a morning excursion without nearly coming to blows. I believe she despises me."

"Surely you are exaggerating. How can any woman despise you, darling?"

He raised one eyebrow. "You are biased, Mother. Utterly and hopelessly prejudiced in my favor—not that I am complaining, mind you. It is just that I know what I know—Imagine how it would be if Miss Fox and I did anything more serious than attend a horse sale. It could be catastrophic!"

"Indeed," Lady Gregory said with a deep sigh. "Catastrophic…"

Chapter 8

"There. I think that should take care of your snarl." Vivian gave the delicate Irish linen square one last pat before she handed the stitching sampler back to Miranda. The thread knots she had sorted out defied description but they made her feel less awkward about the near-disastrous dancing lesson she had just endured. Surely her feet had not gotten nearly as tangled as the threads.

Miranda looked at the scrap of fabric in her hands. She ran a finger across the restored stitches, touching the tiny pleats as if they might dissolve beneath her flesh at any moment.

"You make it look so simple." She threaded her needle with a fresh length of cotton and held it poised above the fabric. "It is almost embarrassing to be so inept—especially at something every woman should do effortlessly."

Lucie, intent on her own work, *tsk-tsked*. "You have plenty of womanly talents. Don't cut yourself short just because pleats come hard to you." Holding her fabric up to the light, she squinted as she inspected the row she had just finished. They were less ungainly than Miranda's were but not nearly as perfect as Vivian's example. With a small, almost delicate sniff she said, "Don't feel bad. You are not the only one who won't be winning any awards for her pleats."

They were seated in the library, beside the wide French doors where the sunlight streamed through the glass and gave plenty of light by which to work. An hour had passed since they left off dancing and began their needlework.

Vivian had never known such pleasant times. Having neither a sister of her own nor the luxury of spare time to cultivate friendships, she had not known what a delight it was to keep female company. The hours she spent with Miranda and Lucie were some of the best she had ever known.

Miranda tossed her sewing aside. "I give up. I know that once I poke that needle into the fabric again I shall make a fresh mess. Since Vivian has just sorted my last bit of chaos out I am going to leave well enough alone. My fingers hurt, anyhow." She scowled at the tips of the fingers on her right hand.

Vivian had noticed the tiny red spots on Miranda's work. "You really need to keep the thimble on, at least until you become familiar with working the needle. Eventually you will build up a callous. See?" Holding up her own finger for inspection, she said, "It is not particularly becoming but it does save me from leaving bloodstains on my sewing."

"I don't know how you do it, Vivian." Lucie set her pleated fabric down on the table beside her chair. She stuck her tongue out at the swatch, and then giggled. "I am hopeless at sewing. Embroidery or crewelwork—even cutwork—I can do, but this heart-and-soul seamstressing is just beyond me. And, while I respect your fine finger, I am sure Nick would not be thrilled if I come home with calluses all over the tops of my fingers. As it is, I am not certain he is going to be thrilled by the little pricks I have given myself poking the needle into my fingers. Goodness, dressmaking is much tougher than I thought it would be!"

When she first met Lucie she had worried the Duchess would be high in the instep and far from approachable but now that they were friends her earlier fears seemed silly. No one could be further from haughty and unsociable than the woman seated nearby.

"I agree." Miranda stuck one index finger in her mouth. Then she added, speaking around the offended fingertip, "And much more painful."

"Oh, you are both too funny! Dressmaking is a skill anyone can learn, if they're willing to put in the time." Vivian shook her head, the memory of the long hours she spent hunched over her sewing never far from her mind. "Eventually it comes naturally, and much more easily. Less painfully, too."

"I shall have to take your word for it. I am not sure I am up to the task. What about you, Lucie?"

"We are not giving up this quickly, Miranda. She will have to find a simpler lesson for us. Perhaps pleats are a bit advanced. We shall have to work up to them, I think. What do you say, Vivian? Will you find something tamer for our next lesson?"

Something tamer?

She scrambled to come up with an interesting project which would guarantee success for everyone. Her mind went momentarily blank before the idea hit her.

"Pockets! Everyone should know how to construct and attach a pocket to the outside of a garment. One can never tell when an extra pocket might come in handy." She glanced at her companions. "What do you think?

Are you up to trying pockets?"

The others exchanged dubious looks. While it seemed that Miranda might refuse, Lucie nodded. Relief washed over Vivian. She wanted them to enjoy their sewing lessons, not to be tortured by them. Pockets were the most rudimentary lesson she could think of—besides hems, which were too boring to consider. No, pockets had at least some appeal and were somewhat useful.

"Pockets it will be," Lucie declared. "As long as they don't have pleats."

"No pleats," Vivian promised. "Now that is settled, I have a request about the next dance lesson."

Miranda frowned. "What is it?"

Miranda had taken her position as dance instructor to heart—perhaps too much to heart. Vivian's toes throbbed painfully inside her kidskin slippers, a testament to the exuberance she had insisted each dancer display.

"No cotillions! I have a headache, trying to recall all the twists and turns of the cotillion you demonstrated earlier. I believe I might have nightmares just thinking about it."

Lucie nodded her agreement. "She is right, you know. No one but you followed any of the dance you were showing us. It did not help that you sent Vivian and I flying through the openings you created between passes and dips."

Miranda sighed. "It probably did not help that I was dancing both parts, did it? Well, I see your point—both of your points." She shrugged, her frown gone and replaced with her usual sunny smile. "No more cotillion lessons. Next time we shall practice the waltz again. It is much more sedate."

"And kinder to the toes." Vivian gingerly rubbed one foot over the other.

She would have loved nothing more than to steal a feature from each of her new friends. It would have made the process of becoming socially adept much more expedient, and substantially simpler.

Miranda, despite her definite leaning toward plumpness, danced like a dream, sweeping across the floor as if borne on the wings of fairies. Once upon a time, long before she knew anything of want or hard work, Vivian had danced in a similar fashion. Of course, the steps were of her own making, the music playing in her mind and her "ballroom" the alley behind the apartment where they lived. Then, she had danced without thought to propriety, with no mind to impressing anyone save herself and with steps so sure she had never stumbled. Her toes had not ached and her pride had remained intact.

Now, the basic steps required for waltzing or the country line dances which were so favored by the upper classes were difficult enough for her to learn. The French cotillion Miranda demonstrated this morning, with its intricate turns and partner changes, was far beyond her rudimentary skills.

Lucie leaned forward, struck a confidential pose and said, "Miranda just likes to show off her cotillion skills. Truly, she does." When her lifelong chum opened her mouth, she cut off the protest. "Do not try to wiggle your way off the hook, duck. You know it is true. You have always been far superior at dancing than I. We all know that if Nick had not taken such a forceful lead during our first dance—which was, unfortunately, a cotillion—I would have made a complete fool of myself. It was only his expert dancing skills that kept me on my feet—and off his toes!"

"Hmmph! You act as if you have two left feet. It is not the case, either for you or Vivian. You both possess adequate physical skills—why, you both can walk and talk at the same time, can't you? Dancing is no different—it is merely a matter of walking to a tune while talking to a handsome—hopefully—partner."

After a fast grin and quick glance at Vivian, Lucie said, "Well, it is a good thing that I have found a husband because it seems that the older I get, the less able I am to coordinate my feet with my mouth."

Shaking her head in amazement, she wished she had a bit of Lucie's fast wit and good humor. Lucie made no attempt to hide her intellectual prowess, something that made its being part of her personality even more likeable than it would have been had she pretended to be less than she truly was.

"You do not seem to have any problems at all." She gazed thoughtfully at the other woman. While Miranda yearned so obviously for a man to call her own, Lucie seemed to lack for nothing. She seemed unreservedly at ease, and fairly glowed with happiness.

What must it take to look so? Vivian wondered if she would ever seem as satisfied as a cat with a bellyful of warm cream. She hoped so, although she did not fully believe it would happen to her.

"Oh, I have problems." A faraway look in Lucie's eyes as she gazed through the French doors and to the sweeping expanse of manicured gardens beyond gave no hint to the thoughts behind the stare. A small shake of her head brought her gaze back to meet Vivian's.

"They are not horribly pressing issues, I grant you, but I don't believe there is anyone on the face of the earth without a tribulation. Or two," she added.

How could she have been so careless? No one was exempt from shouldering some sort of burden.

"I did not mean…why, I am sorry, Lucie. That was insensitive of me to say."

"Don't fret," Miranda said soothingly. She glanced at Lucie. Then, apparently satisfied by what she saw in the other woman's eyes, said, "Lucie and Nick lead a charmed life but that was not always the case. Your relatives have had their share of trials but they have managed to overcome them. And what is on her mind now is something she and Nick will also solve, in their own good time."

Turning to face Lucie, Vivian asked, "Is there anything I can do to help? We are, after all, related. It seems I should share some of the family's misfortunes as well as its good times."

Miranda giggled. Lucie followed her lead. "No, my dear, I am afraid this is one issue Nick and I will have to deal with on our own."

In a loud whisper Miranda said, "They wish to begin a family. They are newly married but His Lordship—"

"Don't call him that! It makes him sound a million years old!" Lucie shot Miranda a disapproving look but it was clear there was no force behind the expression.

As if she had not heard, Miranda continued. "As I was saying, the newlyweds have an eye to the future but there seems little hope of producing an heir when the duke is so frequently away on business. He takes a serious disposition to his business holdings, and seems disinclined to leave the running of his affairs to someone else."

The topic was not one Vivian had discussed before so she wisely kept her lips shut. She did not know about husbands, businesses or babies, so it seemed better not to offer advice.

Lucie did not seem to require any, which was a relief. She did not seem overly Friday-faced by her predicament, because she lifted, then dropped, one shoulder as she smiled.

"I am sure that when the time is right, we will begin our family. Now," she looked over her shoulder toward the closed door. Then, her cheeks pinker than they were only a moment earlier, she said, "I should change the subject. I am sure Mother would have a fit if she heard me speaking of such things with two unmarried women. Why, the scandal it would cause if anyone knew!"

The sound of heels in the hallway brought their conversation to a standstill.

Vivian stared breathlessly at the heavy double doors swung open on silent hinges. Oliver strode into the room as if he owned it—which he did, of course—and put an abrupt end to the female chatter.

Looking every inch the lord of the manor in a navy-blue pinstriped morning coat and severely pleated matching trousers, he bent to kiss Lucie's cheek as he passed her chair. Then, a nod for Miranda.

When Oliver turned to her, Vivian glued a little smile to her face, hoping to conceal the trepidation that had her hands clammy and her throat tight.

Since their outing to the Tattersall horse auction, she had managed to avoid him. It had not been particularly difficult to do so, since the manor house and its grounds were so large they provided ample hiding spots. Not that she was hiding, exactly. No, it was more a case of staying away from the temptation Oliver Gregory brought with his presence. Vivian did not feel tempted by her attraction to him; she had a tricky time resisting the lure to bicker further with the man.

Why does he have to live here?

The thought passed hastily through her mind. She swallowed guiltily as Oliver inclined his head to her, his good manners making her feel bad for having any ill thoughts in his direction. He was, after all, one of her hosts.

"Vivian." His tone was pleasant, and his demeanor suggested a truce.

The white flag of friendship should never be overlooked. With renewed resolve to find common ground with the man before them, she nodded a greeting.

"Oliver. It is…ah, why, it is a nice surprise to see you this morning." There. The sentiment was not entirely true but it was socially acceptable. That, Vivian had come to learn, held much more weight in London circles than the truth did.

"Whatever are you doing inside on such a fabulous day? My dear brother, I would have thought you and Will would be out and about, taking care of something dreadfully important or absolutely pressing." Lucie grinned, raising one impeccably shaped eyebrow in question. "Don't you have something lordly to attend to?"

When Oliver waved a fist in mock threat, the smile

on his face so wide it was almost dazzling in its intensity, she saw a side of him she had not known existed. Love for his sister shone from his eyes and turned his words tender.

"Listen, little sister, just because you are a married woman it does not mean I must take such insults from you. Besides, I could pose the question of Nick's business—is he off on some lordly mission, or is his absence this week due to a more mortal errand?"

"He will only be gone for one night, and it is actually on an errand of mercy."

Sitting heavily on the footstool by his sister's feet, he asked, "Mercy? Whatever do you mean?"

"His friend from school, Charles something-or-other, sent a message and requested Nick's help. I am not certain what the matter is, but I am sure it is one of a financial nature." She lifted one eyebrow as if in surrender, and then went on. "He gets several appeals for monetary help each month. At first I was put off by the sheer volume of them but now I just take it as part of life. Nick does not think those with more than others should hoard their resources. So, he is probably lending a financial hand to his old friend."

"Admirable, but doesn't it bother you that he is spreading the wealth the way he does?" Miranda's eyes opened wide, as if she surprised herself by speaking.

"Not really," Lucie answered. Her gaze touched each of them in turn, and seemed to linger on Vivian. "I agree with him. We have more than enough. Why shouldn't he help those less fortunate?"

Knowing she was technically among the less fortunates of the world made Nicholas Grayson's kindness more meaningful. She knew what it was like to go without, so hearing Lucie and her husband believed in giving help where it was needed struck a chord.

Whatever her differences were with Oliver, these were good, kind people. Vivian counted herself lucky to be in their company.

Oliver smoothed a gentle hand along Lucie's wrist. "When will Nick be home?"

"Tomorrow."

The next was less a question than a statement. "You will be spending the night here, then?"

"You know Father would not have it any other way. Nick, either," Lucie added with a giggle. "Yes, I shall stay. In fact, staying the night will make my excursion with Vivian all the more uncomplicated to carry out."

Vivian sucked in a breath. Her mind had been only half-listening to the conversation, so when she heard her name she was at a loss. The others picked up the thread of dialogue without her help.

"Excursion?" Miranda sat up straighter on the settee, looking a trifle green around the edges. Vivian had not thought her a jealous creature, but if Miranda's glance had been a dagger she would surely be lying on the floor in a bloody heap.

"Do not take on so, Miranda! Why, you look ready to draw Vivian's claret," Lucie said with a small burst of laughter.

Instantly her new friend looked chagrined, turning Vivian's shock at discovering her jealous nature to sympathy. Only a fool—and a blind one, at that— would not see how Miranda felt about Oliver. There were no grand gestures, flowery words or silly machinations, but the subtle clues and longing glances whenever Oliver was near were impossible to miss.

Vivian was so glad she did not want him for her own. High regard for Miranda and her feelings would have made a close association with the man entirely unsuitable. Perhaps he would eventually see what was right before him, the love a sweet woman offered so willingly.

Then, it occurred to her that maybe Oliver did see how Miranda felt. Perhaps her affections did not inspire similar emotions within him.

Who can ever tell the mind of a man? Surely not I, Vivian thought.

When she looked up Oliver was studying her. "An excursion? What exactly do you have up your sleeve, Lucie? I am sure it will fun, whatever it is, but the suspense is turning me inside out. Do tell, please."

A smile played across Lucie's lips. "I have an appointment at Lady Drabble's."

"Lady Drabble's? Surely you jest." Miranda placed a splayed hand upon her bodice, clearly forgetting all about her jealousy as well as the man who, even now, watched her the way a cat might survey a canary. "Why, I have heard she has a waiting list at least four months long, that no one save the most well-heeled is able to gain entrance into her salon. Lady Drabble's— you must be joking!"

Oliver chuckled, but the sound was lost beneath his sister's laughter.

She caught her breath. "Apparently Lady Drabble can find the time to see Mrs. Nicholas Grayson. Honestly, I am not all that overcome by the prospect of a morning in her company but I thought Vivian might enjoy the experience. And you, also, are invited, Miranda. You did not expect I would leave you out, did you?"

Miranda's mouth opened and closed, and she looked like a startled carp thrown to the shore and left gasping for air. She did not speak, but shook her head in denial of the show of jealousy she had demonstrated only minutes ago.

Vivian could not stand the suspense any longer. She did not care that she would look, yet again, socially inept. "For heaven's sake, who is Lady Drabble?"

Oliver held up a hand when his sister tried to answer. He said, in a falsetto voice that was by far the most amusing thing he had done since their initial meeting, "Lady Drabble is the *ton's* most fashionable hairdresser. She is, by all accounts, called frequently to the castle."

The hairdresser to royalty? Shock stilled Vivian's lips. She never imagined being in on an "excursion" to visit the royal hairdresser!

Before anyone could say anything more, the wide double doors flew open and Will rushed in from the hallway. In direct opposition to Oliver's faultless appearance, his cravat was half undone, his breeches wrinkled and his curls wind-blown. The aroma of horseflesh clung to him, permeating the room in a wave that was hard to ignore.

Miranda wrinkled her nose but Vivian's pulse quickened at the sight of Oliver's assistant. It did not matter that his wild-eyed expression merely glanced over her before he caught and held his boss's gaze.

"Well, good morning to you too, Will," Lucie joked.

If he heard her, he did not let on. He looked ready to burst, his lips pulled tight over his teeth and his breath coming in ragged bursts.

"Will? What is wrong?" Oliver stood, crossed the room and took the other man by the shoulders. "Tell me—what is it? You look ready to drop!"

"I have just been to the stables. We have turned them upside down, actually, but there is no sign of her. No sign at all—it is as if she has vanished into thin air. I cannot understand it. Why, she was there just last night but by this morning she was gone—disappeared without a trace." Will sighed, his shoulders falling and an air of disbelief settling over him like a mantle.

"Who?" Oliver spun around, his gaze moving from woman to woman as if he made a silent count. Lord and Lady Gregory were visiting friends for the day, so aside from the household staff Miranda, Lucie and Vivian were the only women at the estate. He turned back to Will. "Who has disappeared?"

Vivian saw the hesitation in his answer, the way he stared at the floor for a long moment before lifting his head and meeting Oliver's questioning eyes.

A feeling of dread—inexplicable and uncontrolled—washed over her. She held her breath, knowing the answer would not bring joy to the room.

"The gray mare, the one you bought at Tattersall's. She is gone from her stall. No one knows where she went, or when she was taken out. None of the stable hands can say who took her." He paused. Then, in a calmer tone of voice, "It is clear she has been stolen. There can be no other explanation for her disappearance, I am afraid."

Seconds before he turned, Vivian knew she was

going to be the first suspect on the list of horse thieves. She knew it, yet could do nothing to prevent the fact.

It was stupid, really. She had never so much as filched a button from an employer, so the idea of her stealing an actual horse was almost incomprehensible. She would no sooner steal a horse than a button—but that, apparently, did not matter to the man who turned to face her.

As she felt the full effect of Oliver's red-hot glare, she realized how snow beneath the sun's rays must feel. Unlike snow, however, she did not melt. Instead, she stood and faced her silent accuser.

She might be a poor relation, but she was no horse thief!

Chapter 9

Lady Drabble and her chamber had been so effusively heralded that when Vivian finally walked into the hallowed hairstyling halls she was completely disenchanted by what she found. This could not be the place where ordinary women became sirens, where fates were sealed by the flip of a curl or the placement of a braid. She looked around, her eyes scanning the space for some sign of the stylist's magic or talent, but found none.

The salon looked utterly, and truly disappointingly, ordinary. Several velvet settees with matching side chairs were scattered in the nearly claustrophobic space. Four large looking glasses lined one wall, and gave a tiny illusion that there was more room in the parlor than there actually was. Tables, some heaped with trailing ribbons, wide-toothed combs and feathers of every size and color, flanked the seats and were the only real evidence of the owner's occupation.

A uniformed maid had shown them in. She dipped a curtsey, departed through a side door and left Vivian, Lucie and Miranda standing in the center of the room. For a long moment, no one spoke. Then, they looked at each other and smiled.

She did not wish to be disrespectful, especially since this treat was designed to impress her, but Vivian could not help herself. She leaned forward, so as not to be overheard even though it seemed they were alone. "Is this what all hairstyling parlors look like? I confess, I have never been inside one before."

"Not what you expected, is it?" Lucie's eyes grew round and her smile broadened. She was such an attractive woman, and her obvious pleasure at their situation made her even more so. Her eyes sparkled, the hair she was to have styled already looked silky and smooth and when she smiled it was as if additional lamps had been lit. Again Vivian was hit by the thought that being near her distant relation was standing in the presence of someone whole-heartedly in love.

"I did not know what to expect." She hoped someday to have the same glow, brought on by unrivaled devotion. "As I said, I have never been inside one of these places so I had no idea what they are like on the inside. This is, I admit, not exactly what I thought it would be."

"Me, either. My hair is usually dressed at home, so this is my first time in a stylist's salon." Miranda reached out and fingered what looked to be some small, dead animal but which was a clump of hair with a large pin attached. Pulling her gloved finger back delicately, she added, "My Abigail has stuck me all over my head countless times over with all manner of hairpins but I have never, thank goodness, worn one of those. I am as game as the next woman for adventure, Lucie, but if Lady Drabble tries to put that on my head I am running for the door!"

Vivian silently seconded the vow. No one, not even one who teased royalty's locks, was going to pin the ratty looking clump of hair on her—not if she had anything to say about it.

She had almost decided against the trip this morning but could not disappoint Lucie by refusing Lady Drabble's attention. It seemed preferable to stay at the manor, by herself, but to be that rude was not something she could do.

Most of the previous night had been spent staring at the ceiling, wondering how much messier her visit might get. So far she had behaved like a social disaster, arrived on the scene just when a burglary was being committed, argued with the man everyone hoped she might enchant and now looked like a thief.

No one had come out and accused her of stealing the gray mare but she knew it had to be on everyone's minds. What else could they think? She had vehemently championed the horse's cause, quarreling with Oliver and spoiling their outing, so it seemed to follow that if anyone had a motive for ferrying the animal away it was her.

While she had not been accused, Vivian still felt the weight of their silent fingers pointing on her.

Before she could fall too low, the same door through which the maid exited opened wide and a rail-thin woman swept into the room. Immediately the air filled with the fragrance of roses, so thick and heavy the scent was almost a cloud hanging over Lady Drabble's head. She rushed to where they stood, threw her arms open wide and silently surveyed them in turn. Finally, she nodded to the maid trailing behind her, gesturing for them all to sit.

She lowered herself onto the edge of the nearest settee, all thoughts of Willowbrook, horses and even Oliver completely turned from her mind.

"You are off for Lady Winter's fete this afternoon,

are you not?" Lady Drabble's deep, hearty timbre sounded strange coming from the small, bird-like woman.

"Yes, we are. I am Lady Grayson, the one who requested your services for the occasion. Thank you for accommodating us, Lady Drabble."

"One does what one must." Her fingernails were long, pointed and sharp-looking, and when she put a finger to her temple and tapped her head thoughtfully Vivian could not help but stare. "Your friends are…?"

"This is Miss Spencer, of London," Lucie said, gesturing with an open hand first to Miranda, then to Vivian. "And this is my cousin, Miss Fox. She is visiting from Stropshire for the Season."

A penetrating stare from the hairdresser. Then, the haughty tone in her voice icy, she said, "Indeed."

Lucie would not be cowed by the woman's apparent dissatisfaction at being called to dress a Stropshire head. She took charge of the situation, sitting up straight and catching the salon owner's gaze.

"I would like you to begin with Miss Fox. Her dress for Lady Winter's party is the loveliest shade of lavender, and will highlight her gorgeous eyes beautifully. They are purple, in case you have not noticed—it is, I believe, one of the Regent's favorite colors, is it not?" She did not wait for Lady Drabble to answer. Vivian watched admiringly as Lucie easily gained the upper hand in the situation. "I am sure you have some spectacular violet ribbon or feather to ornament Miss Fox's natural beauty. It should not be a difficult task to turn her hairdo into something quite fetching—not for a skilled stylist. I trust you will take special care of her, and then fix Miss Spencer's fabulous red locks. Finally, I would like you to dress my own hair up a bit."

Lady Drabble had turned from dragon to bunny rabbit in mere minutes. She nodded meekly, her taloned fingers folded in her lap.

Lucie was not done. She nodded to the tangle of hair and its attached pin. "Oh! One last thing—none of us wish to have anything even remotely resembling that on our heads. Not today. Not ever."

"As you wish, Lady Grayson." The stylist stood, turned to the maid and, in a low voice, requested several brushes. She twisted around to face Vivian, smiling for the first time, and said, "Miss Fox, would you please come this way? The chair beside the looking glass is much more comfortable, and while it will not take long to transform you into a vision I do so want you to be as relaxed as possible."

Vivian could not believe her good fortune. *So this is what it is like to be pampered!*

*****

Oliver smacked his open palm against a horizontal beam on the horse stall. His flesh stung but he did not stop to consider it. He slapped the beam a second time. The horse locked into the stall whinnied, taking a step back with a shake of its mane.

"You are going to scare the devil out of her," Will reached a hand over the beam and nickered softly to the startled animal. He held his hand steady until the horse nudged it with her nose, allowing him to stroke between her eyes while he spoke in a low voice. "She has been through an ordeal. Frightening her will only make whatever has happened worse for her."

Of course Will was right. He usually was, and that

was one of the things he most liked about his assistant. Will could be counted on to provide a reasonable, logical and usually straight-on assessment of any situation. And, equally as important, he told the truth— always.

He slumped forward, placing his arms on the beam he had so recently assaulted and threading his fingers loosely together. To her credit, the horse forgave easily and did not shy away when he moved close.

It galled him to think there was a thief among the residents of the family estate. He hated to believe it, but what other explanation could there be? Since the cottage incident, he had insisted patrols to the all buildings be undertaken by the gardening staff. He had increased his vigilance, riding to all points of the estate without announcing his plans. So far there had been no further break-ins, nothing that seemed even mildly disturbing.

Until this. Horse robbery was not an act to be overlooked—no matter how much he wished he could do so. If their resident bandit had grown as bold as to steal a sixteen-hand horse, what would be next? The manor itself?

"It is too bad she cannot speak." Will's hand made a *shh-ing* sound against the horse's coat. He gave her a gentle pat, then pulled his hand back. "It would make things much easier, wouldn't it?"

Leave it to Will to state the obvious.

Oliver stood silently for a long moment, his gaze on the animal before him.

"How long do you think it would take for you to teach her how to talk? Come on, I know you are capable of almost anything. I have seen you work miracles before. Surely teaching one horse to talk will be effortless for a man of your diverse talents."

Will laughed. The mare whickered but she did not step away. Oliver grinned, his anger giving way to resignation. It was obvious he could not uncover the truth of the horse-napping by staring at the animal, so why give himself a headache over it?

"You flatter me. I assure you, I am not as talented as you seem to believe." Will spread his hands wide, and, addressing the horse, asked, "Where have you been? Pray tell, we are anxious to hear of your escapade." He waited a few beats, then added, "Ah, not talking today, are you? Well, that does not shine a good light on me, does it?"

Oliver laughed, the sensation chasing most of the tension from his shoulders. The situation was almost beyond reason. Theirs had been, for generations, an estate where nothing untoward happened, no one was maligned or taken advantage of and everyone—including the animals—lived in peace and comfort. Suddenly they were in an entirely different state of affairs and he could not think of a way out.

"That woman has brought chaos with her. My dear, distant cousin has created a maelstrom the likes of which this place has never seen before."

Will turned to face him, his brows pulled together so tightly they looked like one furry caterpillar marching across his forehead. "Miss Fox? Surely you cannot truly believe she is responsible for any of what's been going on."

He shrugged. "What else can it be? We were all so calm and quiet here until she fell out of the carriage and onto our doorstep. I hate to think it, but she seems the only one to blame."

"I don't believe it." The refusal was rapid and adamant.

"What else can explain what's been happening? Really, Will—give me one good explanation that does not involve the woman and I will leave off my suspicions. Just one, it is all I ask."

"I wish I could think of something—anything—but nothing comes to mind. Still, I don't believe she is behind all of this." With a wave of his arm, Will took a deep breath and stubbornly set his jaw. A muscle worked in his cheek, throbbing in time with the pulse Oliver saw in his temple.

Recognizing the brick wall when he went up against it was one thing. Leaving off trying to bridge the wall was another. Oliver inhaled, pulling the scent of horse and hay into his lungs. He held it there for a while, considering his words before he spoke. Annoying Will needlessly held no appeal but he could not readily agree his relation was not behind the uproar.

"I cannot think of any other explanation. I would like to think I am not—even distantly—related to a crook—even one as fetching as this one—but no other logical conclusion comes to mind. I am sorry, but that is the truth of it."

Like a dog with a soup bone, Will would not let go of his position. "We have been in some tight spots together, and have seen some unsavory characters in our days, yet—and I know you must agree—we have never, ever met a nefarious character anything like Vivian."

Vivian? Familiarity with anyone except himself was surprising coming from Will. The use of a

Christian name told more than the rest of the conversation just how deep his friend's faith in the charming lady went.

"I do agree." Oliver knew when he was out-maneuvered. It would not hurt to bend on the point, at least for the time being. "Miss Fox—Vivian—is nothing like any of the less-savory types we have met in the past. Still, I would like to know what's been going on since her arrival."

Will patted the horse's neck. "Give me time. Perhaps I can coax this gal into talking, after all."

****

Vivian did not expect William Fulbright to be waiting for her when she went down the manor's wide front staircase before Lady Winter's fete. She did not expect anyone, except perhaps the butler, Hastings. But, as she stepped onto the landing she looked up and saw that Oliver's assistant was, in fact, waiting. He stood when she came into sight, bowing ever-so slightly and smiling up at her.

A jittery sensation skipped through her midsection. She laid a quieting hand across her center, hoping to calm the butterflies that danced beneath her clothing. As she stared down into Will's eyes, she saw unrestrained admiration, and felt lovelier than she ever had.

Beneath Lady Drabble's masterful attention her hair had climbed to heights she did not think it capable of achieving. Intricate twists and curls, all held in place by hidden hair pins, had turned her ordinary hair truly spectacular. One discreet thread of amethyst beads ran through the hairstyle, perfectly matching the color of her dress as well as complementing her violet eyes.

First impressions had been false where the hairstylist had been concerned. Her vision and proficiency were unrivaled. All three women had emerged from her humble parlor with beautifully coiled locks and, more importantly perhaps, each looked unique.

Vivian descended the staircase, deep breaths accompanying her every step. She did not know why she suddenly felt wobbly-kneed, only that she did. When she reached the bottom, she took one last deep breath before she met Will Fulbright's gaze.

He swept a magnificent leg, and then straightened. "You look lovely, Miss Fox."

Such pomp. And for her, someone whose pedigree was less impressive than that of almost any household staff member!

It took a moment to respond. She could not think past the butterflies once again waltzing in her tummy.

"Thank you. That is very kind of you to say, Mister Fulbright."

She swallowed hard, and hoped that neither Hastings, who stood a discreet distance from them, beside the front door, nor the man who flattered her so could hear the hammering of her heart. On her side, it felt like the organ in question was actually trying to pound its way out of her chest. Surely something that forceful must be audible to ears other than hers!

When neither man gave any hint that they could, in fact, perceive the sound of her thudding heart, Vivian grew bolder. She curtsied, careful not to catch the hem of her gown beneath the toe of a dainty kidskin slipper.

She smiled as she rose, the expression needing no conscious effort.

"I assure you, I was not merely being kind. I…" He stared into her eyes so deeply and for so long Vivian felt connected to him in a way that was both startling and exhilarating. His examination was neither rude nor probing, but she felt he saw past the trappings of society—even her royalty-inspired hairdo—to the woman beneath the frills.

His pause lengthened, and since he did not seem put off by what stood before him, she leaned closer and asked, "You were about to say something?"

Clearing his throat, he broke their connection. "I…ah, yes. I was just going to say that my compliment was not a bit of Spanish coin; it is the truth—you are exquisite this afternoon, Miss Fox. I am certain you will shine down every other lady at the fete, including Lady Winter herself." He grinned boyishly, waggling his eyebrows up and down dramatically. "But I shall deny that statement if you tattle on me. Lady Winter is notoriously conscious of her appearance, you know."

"Aren't we all?"

He cocked his head, taking his time replying. Just when Vivian began to wonder what was on his mind, he said, "Are you? Why, you don't seem at all the type to be preoccupied by looks or any of the other 'usual' societal trappings."

How had he pegged her so neatly? Was she that transparent?

"Are you this bold with every woman you meet, or am I someone who does not inspire propriety? Because, it seems even to me, someone with limited social schooling, that your observation and question are wholly improper, Mister Fulbright." Her hackles rose of their own accord, and her mouth had not given warning that it was about to erupt. When the words tumbled out, Vivian was appalled. Clapping a hand over her lips, she stared at her escort in abject horror.

A quick glance at Hastings confirmed her suspicions that her response had not been any more proper than the man's probing. The butler's lips twitched, but he did not smile. She turned her attention back to the man standing before her.

Now I have done it! There will be the devil to pay for my reckless remarks!

Will chuckled, the sound deep and rich and entirely unexpected. He gave her a tiny bow, placing a hand over his heart. "You have me there. I did speak without thinking, and I apologize. Please do not hold my brashness against me. It is just that you are so completely unlike any other woman we have had stay at the manor, so wonderfully unaffected and seemingly unfettered by so many of society's stupid rules that I cannot help but be taken by your refreshing qualities. Again, I am speaking without leave. I have no right to be 'taken' by you at all but there is no help for it. You are enchanting, and certain to catch every eye at the fete."

Swallowing hard, she nodded her acceptance of his apology and ventured to give him a small smile. "By all means, Mister Fulbright, be as 'taken' as you care to be."

****

The landau offered a smooth, pleasant ride. Its wide facing seats provided the ideal arrangement. Vivian was near enough her escort to feel comfortable but not so near his proximity put her off. Occasionally their knees bumped, and once they had hit a particularly deep rut that had sent her jostling forward which necessitated his catching her by the shoulders to steady her but there had been no untoward contact.

The touch—ever-so fleeting—of his hands on her shoulders had heated her skin more than the bright orb shining down on them did but Vivian was careful not to show the fact. She could not afford to bring more gossip down on her head. Already the manor must be buzzing with stories of how she and her escort had behaved before heading to the party. Giving more material for the servants' wagging tongues was not something she was prepared to do, so she was supremely mindful that their driver had ears, and was most likely listening to every spoken word.

At first she had been surprised to hear that Oliver had sent his assistant to accompany her to the party. She had thought to go on her own, but now realized that would have been scandalous. So many rules to keep straight—they nearly gave her a headache when she tried to keep the 'must' list separate from the 'must-not' column in her head.

Lady Winter's London home was not far, but the driver seemed in no hurry to convey them so the horses clip-clopped at a sedate speed. Now and then a breeze lifted a curl from Vivian's neck but she did not worry her style would come undone. There were far too many hairpins in her tresses for that to happen, so she sat back against the white leather seat and enjoyed the ride.

"Do you miss Stropshire? Or your family?"

His questions were like a slap on her cheek. They pulled her attention from the passing scenery, bringing a fresh wave of homesickness. Vivian had not let on that she yearned for her mother and brother, not wishing to seem ungrateful for the Gregory's gracious hospitality.

The eyes boring into hers did not seem capable of hurting anyone, so she did not dissemble.

"I do not miss Stropshire all that much, or our little flat, either. They are all good and well as far as being somewhere decent to live, but now that I have seen a bit of Town I am more of a mind to think I would prefer to live near London. And of course our tiny walk-up is nothing by comparison to the grandeur of Willowbrook Manor." She paused, watching a pair of sparrows light in the low branch of a passing oak. Even the birds in this part of England seemed content. Meeting the gaze of the man seated across from her, Vivian shrugged. "I know I will never live anywhere nearly as impressive as Lord and Lady Gregory's estate again, but I would like to end up somewhere that is quiet, peaceful and is near enough to the city that I might take part in some of the cultural activities."

"Such as?"

Chagrined, Vivian lifted her shoulders again, tightening her grip on the parasol she held above her head. "I am not sure, exactly, which activities I would enjoy most. Certainly I have no aspirations to attend balls, fetes or lush lawn parties. In moderation, or for special occasions, they are beguiling but I do not believe I could stand a steady diet of them."

His laughter was so genuine it did not make her feel she had put her foot in it again. Telling the truth to the man came naturally, and she had spoken without thinking but there was no censure in his merriment so she smiled.

"You are charming, Miss Fox."

"Thank you, Mister Fulbright."

A tilt of his head, and a thoughtful look inspired her to ask, "What are you thinking?"

"It is just that I feel closeness between us, an openness that makes hearing the formal form of address seem incongruous. I know, it is a necessary societal evil but still, I would much prefer you might call me by my given name." He lifted one eyebrow in question.

It was unthinkable, and would surely set tongues on fire so she gave her head a vehement shake. Opening her mouth to refuse, but not knowing precisely how to do so made her feel foolish so she snapped her lips together and shook her head again.

Chuckling, he nodded. "I thought that would be your answer but you cannot shoot a man for attempting to form an association, can you?"

"Of course not, Mister Fulbright."

"That, at least, is something." He pointed to the street sign on the corner as they came abreast of it. "Gorham Square. We are nearly there, and you have not yet answered my question. Do you miss your family, Miss Fox?"

"Very much, I am afraid. It is the only gray spot on this trip, my missing Mother and Liam the way I do." A sheen of unshed tears clouded her vision. "We are a small family, but we are close. I have been treated as a member of the Gregory family from the moment of my arrival but…"

"It is not the same, is it?" His tone was gentle.

"No," she whispered. "It is not the same at all." It would not do to arrive at Lady Winter's with tear-stained cheeks, so Vivian forced herself to smile. She looked up, into the dark brown eyes that gazed at her so kind and caring they warmed her heart. "What about you? Do you miss your family?"

Mister Fulbright shook his head. "No, I don't. I am fortunate enough to see them often—every week, in fact. I have a small cottage near Oliver's—ah, near Lord Gregory's cottage—and I have two Sundays and several afternoons a month free so I either have my family to visit or I take one of the carriages and go to Town to visit them. It is a suitable arrangement for all, one that I know I am fortunate to have."

"Do you have a large family?" Her interest was genuine. She imagined him surrounded by brothers and sisters, with doting parents and scads of aunts, uncles and cousins. The way he fitted effortlessly into any situation gave her the impression that his adaptability had been a trait learned early on.

"I do, actually. Three brothers, two sisters and so many cousins that I cannot count them all."

"I knew it."

"You did? How could you possibly know?" He held one hand, palm up and open to the brilliant blue sky, and asked, "Do you read minds, Miss Fox?"

She brushed aside the notion with a giggle. How lovely it was to feel so light-hearted!

"Hardly. It was purely a guess, one I based on your demeanor. You are so easy-going; it is not hard to imagine you surrounded by a big, loving family." They were passing a hedge of white lilacs, and when she sighed, pulling air deeply into her lungs, she became almost intoxicated by the sweetness of the blooms. "It is…"

"It is what?"

What harm could there be in telling the secrets of

her heart, especially to a man who seemed so capable of keeping them?

"A big family…it is just what I have wished for all my life." Lifting her gaze to his, she added, "It is what I hope to find someday for myself—a home filled with children…and with love."

He reached for her free hand where it lay on her skirt, covering it with one of his own. His touch was electric, a sizzling sensation that traveled from his fingers to hers, then up to the point in her chest where her heart once again thrummed madly.

The touch was too forward by far but Vivian was much too surprised to pull away. Moreover, the feelings his fingertips inspired were too lovely by far to needlessly curtail.

His voice was low, too low for the carriage driver to hear. Gazing into the kind eyes that held her gaze, Vivian knew the words he spoke were meant only for her ears.

"You are so sweet, Vivian, that I have no doubt you shall someday find your home filled with laughing children, and your heart taken by one very lucky man."

She was stunned, but managed a reply. "And you …you shall find someone suitable as well. I, ah, imagine it is fortuitous that your position is so high— ah…brotherly, even, in connection with Oliver." She shook her head and struggled to find the correct words. He had just offered a grand compliment, and here she was, stammering like fool.

"That is so. It is unusual, I know, to be elevated from hired help to stand-in-brother, but it is not the first time it has happened." He ran a palm across his cheek. "The life of a peer is unique, and affords one substantial leeway in many areas—despite the rules of convention. It is my good fortune to find myself in this position, thanks to your relation's brotherly affection for me, as well as his family's prominence which brooks no dispute among his peers. Without that, I would be unable to accompany a beautiful woman on such a lovely outing."

Vivian was too stunned for words.

The driver called over his shoulder, "We have arrived at Winterdale."

Chapter 10

After the stimulating—and incredible—ride, the fete itself seemed dull by comparison. An assortment of faces, some recognizable from the last party as well as the few trips to Town and St. George's Church for Sunday services, popped into view as Vivian made her way through the crowd. She did not speak to anyone, choosing instead to smile, nod or, when absolutely necessary, bob a fast curtsey.

Each time a servant brought a tray filled with sweets or punch to her attention, she declined with a small shake of her head. Studiously avoiding the banquet tables like they were covered with rodents instead of refreshments insured she would not make the scandalous mistake of eating in public a second time.

A voice at her ear caught her attention. Vivian whirled around and found herself nearly nose-to-nose with Miranda. She grinned, relief at seeing a friendly face almost compelling her to act—yet again!—more like a Haymarket ware than a lady. She was neither, of course, but fortunately more aligned with the second example than the first so she settled for grasping one of Miranda's hands.

"Are you enjoying yourself?"

"I am, although I have not seen anyone I am nearly friendly with since I arrived. That is, until you showed up."

Miranda looked stunning, her hair done up in countless miniscule ringlets piled all over her head. A few dangled beside her left cheek, a deep blue satin ribbon tied just above the cascade of fiery red curls. She looked like an Irish princess, and would have looked even more so had her dress been green instead of blue.

It occurred to Vivian that she had never seen her new friend wear anything but blue.

"Do you wear anything else?" The absurdity of her question made her giggle. "Oh, that sounds completely half-witted, doesn't it?"

Miranda nodded, a smile making her look even prettier. "It does sound silly but don't worry. I know just what you are trying to ask."

"You are not offended?" The line between propriety and insult was fuzzy, even after the lessons Miranda and Lucie had given her.

"Pish posh! Of course I am not put out in the least. It takes much more than a little query to ruffle these feathers." Emphasizing her words with a flutter of the teal blue fan she held near the lace ruffled on her bodice, she said, "You want to know if I wear any color other than blue. I know that is your question, and the answer is no, I do not. Blue is my signature color, you see. I have always worn it, almost since I was in leading strings. It sets me apart from everyone else, I think."

The notion amused Vivian but she refused to let her feelings show. Miranda looked so earnest that even the tiniest smirk might hurt her feelings, and that was something she was not going to risk. She shook her head solemnly, as if in complete agreement.

Miranda swept a hand down the front of her skirt. "I need a signature color, you see. It keeps me one step removed from the rest of the pack, if you will. But you, of course, need no such artifice. You, dear Vivian, are an original—and wholly on your own."

Almost afraid to ask what made her so unique but unable to resist finding out, she leaned close so no one else would hear. "Ah...would you—I mean, could you please tell me *what* exactly sets me apart? I have tried so desperately, as you are aware, to fit in that if there is something I am missing I would like to be apprised of my foible, if only so I may fix myself."

Miranda shook her head, a huge smile lighting her face. "You cannot fix what is not broken. Why, I did not mean there is anything about you that needs to be changed. I am sorry if I gave you that impression."

Botheration! How can anyone tell what these people are thinking when they do not speak plainly?

"What then?" She forced her features to remain bland even though her pulse raced. Confusion was not one of her favorite emotions, but it was one she felt often as of late. "What is it that sets me apart—and can I do anything about it?"

Miranda rubbed a fingertip across Vivian's gloved knuckles, the gesture as soothing as one given to calm a nervous child. "You cannot change the attribute I refer to no matter how hard you try. And I cannot believe you are so naïve that you do not realize your own beauty...why, your eyes—their color unlike any I have ever seen on anyone in my entire life—sets you apart so distinctly that no woman can come close to your beauty in that area. Your violet eyes are unrivaled, and put you head-and-shoulders above the rest of us ordinary females in that yours are the first eyes any man will notice."

Ah, the eyes again. The one legacy of her father's that brought any attention at all.

A relationship with the man, rather than the inheritance of his astounding eye shade, would have been far preferable. Since that dream would never come to fruition Vivian resigned herself to her sole connection with the man she never knew, and smiled her understanding. Telling Miranda she would gladly trade purple eyes for a hint of a tie with her father would only bring undue attention to the fact that her father was not part of her life.

"Thank you for the compliment. I have never thought much about my eyes, and did not realize they are so unusual. They are eyes, and I am grateful they serve their purpose."

Miranda stared at her for a long minute. "It must be nice to be able to wear extravagance as if it is nothing extraordinary. You do it well, you know."

"Again, I appreciate the compliment." She cast her gaze at the splendor around her. Extravagance changed according to one's perspective. She tilted her head to the dance floor, where lines for a country dance were being formed amidst giggles and conversation. "But I must say that I think we have differing views of...well, of extraordinariness. My eyes arrive in my head through no conscious decision; they are just there and I can either like them or not. Honestly, I am not that taken with them—as I said, they serve their purpose." She swept an open hand toward the room, to the dancers who had begun moving in time to the musicians' notes. "Now this is extravagance, and much more pronounced than a set of eyes."

Regarding the scene in silence, Miranda did not

answer immediately. Vivian watched, and saw her friend's eyes widen. She turned to the doorway, and saw what had caught the other woman's attention.

Oliver and Will stood side by side in the open doorway. They spoke with their hostess, Lady Winters, who was so busy tittering and waving a lace-edged handkerchief at Oliver that she seemed not to notice the man beside him.

Watching someone ignore Will brought a pang of annoyance to Vivian's moment. Then, she saw Oliver put a hand on his companion's arm and draw him into the conversation. Even from a distance it was obvious that Lady Winters turned at least a portion of her attention to Will.

Vivian released a pent-up breath.

"This comes in much the same fashion as your eyes." Miranda took one step closer, and spoke softly near Vivian's ear. "I have done nothing to gain entrance into this world. It is a gift of birth—like one's eyes or nose—and even if it does not astound me I must deal with it on a daily basis. Truthfully, I would much prefer gorgeous eyes than endless rounds of mundane conversation, silly posturing and being surrounded by people who rarely—if ever—say precisely what is on their minds. That is one of the things I admire most about you, you know. You always say what you are thinking, and leave no guesswork. It is refreshing, and I could quite get used to having you around."

She had no intention of staying with Lord and Lady Gregory past the end of the Season. "You should not grow too accustomed to my face, I am afraid. I do not plan to stay on in London for too much longer."

"Are you certain? You will not stay on, not even

if—well, not even if someone were to give you reason to linger?"

She watched Oliver and Will enter the room and begin to mingle with the other guests above Miranda's shoulder. There was no denying Oliver Gregory's dashing good looks or his forceful presence. He stood out in a crowd, not solely due to his appearance but to the countenance that surrounded him. It was clear he was a man who knew his station in life and what the future held for him. He fit into society as perfectly as a finger into a custom-made glove.

But it was not Oliver who held her attention, or set her heart fluttering. It was not Will's looks—although they were highly favorable—that kept her focus. Beneath the polished exterior and casual features, Will was the embodiment of everything she held in highest regard. He had a grasp of what she had always called the Three F's—faith, family and friendships. They were the items which mattered most to her, and she believed Will held them equally dear.

If only Will were Lord and Lady Gregory's heir instead of his assistant. How trouble-free her life would be if that might be the case.

But Will Fulbright is not Lord Gregory's son, Vivian reminded herself with a stern shake.

"It does not matter who asks what of me. I have no plans to remain in London after the close of the Season. It is fun being here, and while I enjoy these parties and the chance to wear fancy clothes, this is not my life. This time has been intended as a lark, but I must return to my world, to my family and the work I do."

"Nothing, then, could entice you to delay leaving?"

Vivian met her gaze. "Nothing. And no one. No

one—not even Oliver Gregory." She gave the declaration a moment to sink in. "I am not hedging when I say he and I have no feelings for each other. We never will, regardless of what my mother and his would like. It is the truth, my friend. I would not play you false."

Miranda clasped her in a fast hug before she stood back and smoothed down the ruffles on her blue dress. "I am sorry your weeks at the Marriage Mart have not worked out, but it is no secret I am glad no one has yet claimed Oliver's affections." She sighed, and Vivian felt instantly sorry for her.

"Come, let us look for Lucie." Grabbing Miranda's hand and pulling her in what was most certainly an unacceptably exuberant manner toward the wide French doors leading onto a terrace, she said, "She is sure to be doing something more interesting than we are. Why, dangling about for a man hardly makes it worth having Lady Drabble do our hairstyles, does it?"

****

"Her feet are as long and wide as boats." Oliver rubbed the toe of one boot against the calf of his other leg, teetering slightly as he stood on one foot. "It is no wonder she had an empty dance card. I must be the only one fool enough to partner her."

Will snorted, grinning above the rim of his punch glass. "Oh, come on, Miss Brougham cannot dance all that badly."

"Count yourself lucky that you do not have the misfortune of being among her eligible dance partners. She is, most assuredly, the least refined dancer I have ever met. And, as you well know, I have danced with enough women to know a fleet-footed one from—well, let us just leave it at that. If you see Miss Brougham so much as peering in my direction, you must warn me, Will. I will not dance with her again—my toes cannot take the abuse."

"As you wish."

"I wish," Oliver growled.

The party had been going so well until he had been cornered by the earl's daughter. Selene Brougham was comely enough, and could hold a general books-and-weather conversation, but beneath her pretty skirts hid weapon-like feet. The memory of their waltz made him shudder.

With the festivities brought an opportunity to speak with nearly all of the men he had invited to the upcoming fox hunt at the manor. It was only a week hence, and he was satisfied to learn that everyone planned to attend. His parents would be pleased when he passed the news on to them.

"It will be good to host an affair, don't you think?" Oliver drained his punch glass and set it on a passing servant's tray. "The hunt should be a good time, even if I am not of a mind to catch the fox myself."

"Why, it would be in poor taste for you to corner her. There is no pressure on you to chase her down, so you should just be able to enjoy the day."

Leave it to Will to see the heart of things. Oliver's distaste for hunting had almost made him cancel the event more than once. It would have disappointed his father so he had not done so but every time he checked on the little red fox penned in the far end of their stable he felt guilty.

"That is what I keep telling myself," he muttered.

Oliver scanned the crowd, hoping for some sign of

his sister and her friends. The day grew long and he hoped to leave shortly. A large barouche waited to take them back to the estate. Between the recent thefts and upcoming hunt, he had much to do and planned to leave sooner rather than later.

If only he could find the women…

A lesser earl and his young son pushed roughly past him. Another man might have caused a fuss but one look at the men showed they had imbibed more than punch, so Oliver let their rudeness pass. He kept his face to the crowd, looking for the three women.

"There they are." Will nodded toward the edge of the crowd, where Lucie, Miranda and Vivian stood laughing. "Over by the column, beside the doorway."

"I see them."

The earl's son must have seen them, as well. He poked his father in his fleshy midsection and said in a slurred voice, "Look there, Father. That one might have v-v-vi—she might have purple eyes but she sure is a green girl."

There were numerous less-flattering remarks the inebriated fool could have made. Calling Vivian young and inexperienced, while rude, was not reason for calling him out.

Before he could manage a word of reproach, Will reached out and spun the startled young man about.

"Silence," Will spat. "You are foxed, and should keep your mouth shut." Leaning close, his voice a hoarse growl, he gave the man one small shake by the front of his jacket as he said, "If I hear you talk crudely about a lady—any lady—again, I will do more than shake you. Understood?"

The earl watched, his mouth hanging wide. When

he seemed about to protest, Oliver shot him a warning look. It did not matter that Will was his assistant and the man he had in hand was a peer. It did not matter one bit, and he was not about to give anyone else the chance to protest.

"Understood." The reply was meek, its owner substantially subdued.

Chapter 11

"Nick and I met at one of Lady Winters's affairs, you know."

Lucie and Vivian sat side on one of the barouche's long, wide black leather seats. Will and Oliver faced them. Both had been strangely silent during most of the trip. Vivian had kept up her side of the conversation, responding to Lucie's comments and answering questions while she wondered what kept the two men so quiet.

She hoped she had not somehow made a cake of herself again. Vivian skimmed through memories of the conversations she had been part of, the dances she had enjoyed and all the scrumptious food she did not sample. *What could I have done now? My behavior was surely beyond notice...wasn't it?*

A soft tap on her thigh brought her back to the present. Lucie grinned at her, as if she knew Vivian had been thinking of something else entirely.

"Yoo hoo, Vivian...are you with us?"

"I did not mean to let my mind wander." The day had been lovely, but it had been long and she was tired. Not sleeping much the night before did not do much for her concentration, either. "I was just...ah, I was only thinking back onto the fun we just had. It was a very enjoyable party."

"Perhaps Vivian found someone at the party who

caught her attention." Oliver's tone was teasing. "Who knows? The man of her dreams might have made himself known to her today."

She glanced at him, mentally begging him to keep his thoughts to himself. Will frowned—she did not know why he did, only that she did not wish to have any of her early conversation, the confidences she had shared on the ride to the party, brought to light now.

"I do not have a dream man." She wished her corset was not tied so tightly. Suddenly she felt she could barely catch her breath.

"What else could be so engrossing?" When Oliver smiled, leaning forward to place his elbows on his knees and staring into her eyes, she almost knew how it must feel to have an older brother. They were past the point of arguing—thankfully—and now that they both had made it quite clear they did not feel any romantic stirrings for each other there was a much more casual tone to their exchanges. "Hmm?"

"Do not tease so." Lucie tapped him lightly on the knuckles with her closed fan. "Poor Vivian is not your sister, and does not have to put up with your silliness. I have endured it all my life, but she does not have to do so. Remember, you may torment me but everyone else is exempt, dear brother."

"I do not mean to torment, and I think she knows that. Why, I am only asking if anyone has caught her fancy. What harm is there in that?"

Oliver pasted such an honest expression his face that he looked almost comical, like a naughty schoolboy pretending not to have a frog in his pocket.

Vivian laughed, unable to take umbrage with the good-natured prodding.

"No one has caught my fancy," she said quickly. "At least, no one I wish to discuss this moment with you."

"Aha! I knew it! Someone has caught your eye." He turned to the man beside him. "Will—did you hear that? Our Vivian has met someone!"

How had the conversation gotten so convoluted so quickly? She could hardly keep up with the threads as they spun wildly out of control, and wished in that moment that she was still daydreaming and had kept her thoughts to herself.

"Stop it—why, you are horrid, Oliver, teasing Vivian this way. Do not try to pull dear Will into your antics. He is much too kind a gentleman to fall for your tricks."

Turning to Vivian, her gaze deliberately off the two men, Lucie said, "As I said earlier, before the shenanigans erupted, Nick and I met at one of Lady Winters's functions. It was a charity event, and while we did not speak much past the introduction we certainly made an impression on each other." Sitting back against the carriage seat and crossing her arms over her chest, Lucie stared up at the leather top stretched above them and sighed. "It was romantic, and I suppose we shall always be in Lady Winters's debt. Without her charity luncheon who knows how long it would have taken for Nick and I to find each other?"

Little seemed to be called for but she murmured, "Who knows? It might have been ages."

"My thoughts exactly," Lucie answered. "I do hope Nick is waiting for us at the manor when we arrive. It has only been a day since I saw him last, yet it feels like an eternity…"

"True love," Oliver said, a chuckle in his voice. "Why, little sister, who would have thought you would turn so romantic? All your life you have been so sensible, and here you are as wobbly as a bowl of pudding. Have you ever seen such a thing, Will?"

The small smile playing around the edges of Will's lips gave Vivian a jolt of pleasure. She smiled in return, and felt her cheeks flush when his smile grew broader.

"Will? Are you daydreaming as well? Why, am I the only one in this carriage whose head isn't lost to Cupid's arrow or some—hold up." Oliver leaned out of the carriage window and yelled a second time to the driver. "Hold up, I say. Stop!"

Astonishment hit her like a bucket of ice water. The carriage screeched to a halt and Oliver, giving no explanation for his incredible behavior, threw the side door open and leapt from the conveyance.

For a second, no one moved. Then, Will followed Oliver, leaving the women alone to stare at each other.

"Whatever is going on?" Vivian held a hand over her heart, but it did nothing to stop the thudding beneath her touch.

"I have no idea." Lucie gathered her skirt in her hand and moved to the doorway. "But I intend to find out."

Wordlessly Vivian followed. She stood beside Lucie, next to the carriage and looked at the scene before them. It looked and sounded unreal, like something from a theatre production. A comedy of errors perhaps, or some ragtag social commentary.

"Let go! I tell you, let go of me!"

"What do you think you are doing?" Will held the reins of a horse, one instantly recognizable. It was the gray mare—the one that had so recently gone missing. "Where are you taking this horse?"

"Confess! Confess now and things will go better for you," Olivier roared.

He held a small figure so tightly by one arm that the toe of one foot was off the ground. He gave a shake, bellowing orders like an enraged bull.

"Will, tie the animal to the back of the carriage. Boy, tell the truth! If you do not come clean I will have you to the constable so fast you won't know how you got there."

"Let me go!" The figure—she could see now that it was a boy—tried to wriggle free. "Let me go!"

Vivian had never seen a man so enraged. Oliver frightened her—until she caught a glimpse of the face attached to the small body he shook so easily. She rushed forward, put her hand on Oliver's arm and tugged as hard as she could. He was all muscle beneath his jacket, and gave no indication he felt her presence.

"Oliver!" Lucie shouted, running to stand beside Vivian. She placed her hand above Vivian's, higher on her brother's arm, and pulled to claim his attention. "You must calm down. Please!"

"I will calm down when this ruffian reveals himself, and not before!"

Will had been busy tying the horse to the carriage. Now he rushed forward and held the child by the other arm. His presence, and grip, made shaking the boy impossible so at least that stopped.

"Let me go!"

"Wait—you are the climbing boy." Will looked to the other man. "He was at the house a few days ago with the chimney sweep."

"Let me go." The child tried to kick Oliver in the shins but he did not hit his mark.

"Oliver—let him go!" Vivian had never yelled before, but she gave every bit of strength she had to pushing the sound from her throat. "It is Eddie, the climbing boy. You must let him go!"

Something—be it his sister's begging, his assistant's presence or Vivian's words—got through because he loosened his grip on the boy. Turning to face her, he sneered, "Eddie? Is he one of your cohorts, then? A little thief sent to do what might be noticed by one larger than he?"

"Oliver!" Lucie's outrage sliced through the dusk, silencing the clamor. "How could you say such a thing?" She reached for Vivian, and would have put an arm around her shoulders but Vivian could not stand the thought of anyone touching her. She twisted away, out of reach, and pretended not to see the hurt expression on the other woman's face.

Even the boy had stopped struggling. He watched intently, his gaze going from one to the other of them. She managed a small smile at him, and a nod, and hoped he might see she would do all she could to help him—despite the maligning of her character.

Keep your chin up, child. Her mother's voice echoed in her head. For as long as she could recall, every time Vivian had stumbled or felt sad, her mother had implored her to keep her chin high and move forward. They were words to live by, so she straightened her spine and took a deep, steadying breath.

She chose to ignore Oliver's implication. Giving him any response could only demean her further, and she was far too worn out to trade barbs with him. All the joy she had felt just a short time ago had vanished, a wisp swept off on a stiff summer breeze.

"He is only a child," she said with as much dignity as she could muster. "I cannot imagine that a climbing boy might pose such an enormous threat to as wealthy a family as yours but I do suspect that one shaken—and possibly wounded—little boy would bring scandal to Willowbrook. Your parents would hate that, I am sure, so I advise you to let the boy go. You are hurting him, I am sure."

She waited until Oliver's grip loosened and Eddie wrenched his arm out of its bondage. When the child took a step back, she did the same.

The thought that they all stared at her brought her nearly to tears—but she would not allow herself to cry in front of these people. They were horrid, the whole lot of them, and deserved no further display at her expense. She could think of nothing but escape, and would have run had she not known it would make her look as guilty as the young horse thief.

Oh yes, she knew in her heart that, for whatever reason, little Eddie was stealing the gray mare. And while she knew, she did not care. Not about the horse, or about anyone present. They would have to sort themselves out. All Vivian wanted was to go home to Stropshire as quickly as possible.

Turning on her heel, Vivian began to walk down the lane. Fortunately they were only a half-mile or so from the manor, so the trek would not be arduous. From behind her, Lucie's voice called her back but she did not turn. Walking, with its steady beat and mindlessness, was as much as she could handle, so it was all she did. She put one foot in front of the other and hoped she did not stumble. Having to be rescued from the lane by any of them would certainly be more than she could bear.

Keep my chin up. Keep my chin up, and find my way home.

****

"You know we are sorry—all of us, for everything. Mother says she spent most of last night trying to convince you to stay. Oh, Vivian, don't you see? We did not mean any harm!"

Lucie's hands clasped over her heart, and her tone was so distressed that had she not been so determined to leave without shedding any more tears she would have given in and stopped packing. It was true; Lady Gregory had stood almost precisely where her daughter stood now, in the room that once was Lucie's and had explained, time and again, just how awfully sorry they all were for the misunderstanding.

Eddie and his father, who had gone into the cottage after finding a window blown in, the victim of a falling branch, had confessed to the minor thefts that had taken place at the estate. They had returned the horse after the first theft, feeling the burden of their actions, but had little choice but to steal her again when their situation grew direr.

Unfortunately their reduced circumstances had come at nearly the same moment of Vivian's arrival, and had made her seem the only suspect in the "rash" of wrongdoings. They had explained that they used the horse to go to the doctor for medicine for Eddie's mother, and that they had "borrowed" blankets from the cottage to keep her warm. Even the missing pail of milk from the barn and a half-bushel of beans had been pilfered by the pair with the hope of letting an ailing woman regain some strength.

Eddie and his family were now comfortably ensconced in one of the apartments in the servants' wing. Both the boy and his father had been offered employment on the estate, something that would be offered to the child's mother when she was able to work again. The men were slated to begin their jobs by helping with the upcoming fox hunt, something Eddie, when he had come to apologize to Vivian, had been very excited about.

Everyone had apologized, but Vivian did not care. Lord and Lady Gregory and Lucie were upset by her insistence on leaving but they would get over it eventually. Oliver had practically torn his hair out, he was so distraught at his jumping to the wrong—and, he insisted, most grievous—conclusions. He had spoken without thinking, in the heat of the moment and was, she knew, truly contrite.

Still, she was set on leaving. It was the only way to regain some of her old life—and untangle the roiling emotions threatening to burst from her.

She shook her head. "It does not matter. I see that no one meant any harm, but the fact is that harm has been done. I need to go home. I do not belong here."

"But we are family—"

"This isn't my world. I-I-oh, I just cannot stay."

A tear slid down Lucie's cheek. "If you insist."

"I do. I am sorry, but I have to leave."

****

Vivian arrived in disgrace, in a wretched carriage reeking of body odor, garlic and stale smoke.

The Gregorys insisted on sending her back to Stropshire in one of their carriages, and would not hear of her refusing them. Vivian ran a hand along the sleek leather seat beside her, inhaled the sweet scent of lavender from the sachets swinging beside the open windows and shook her head.

She was departing in style, so why did she feel so wretched?

She sat back against the seat, sighing heavily. What had started out as a lark had turned into a nightmare. The sting of yesterday's confrontation, the knowledge that despite her best efforts Oliver had thought her capable of thievery, sent a profound wave of sadness washing over her. She could barely breathe.

That is not the worst of it, she thought, hitching a breath. Now that she was alone, and would be for many miles, gave her leave to let down her guard. A sniff, and then a shimmer of wetness on her eyes matched the lump forming in her throat.

They did not know me. They did not trust me. They did not—

A male voice reached her through the open windows. "Stop. I say, stop the carriage this very instant!"

The carriage wheels slowed. Then, they stopped turning.

"That's right—stop the carriage!" The voice was familiar but before she could even sit up and look toward the sound, one of the doors swung open and Will climbed inside.

His hair stood up in waves and dust covered his breeches, shoes and the white shirt he wore unbuttoned at the neck. Always before he had appeared so starched and proper. Now it was a shock to see him in such dishabille.

"You cannot leave."

He smelled of horse when he slid onto the seat beside her. His thigh brushed hers, pushing her back into the corner against the wall of the carriage. Will filled the space beside her so fully that Vivian felt breathless, her pulse tripping and her thoughts jumbled.

She said the first thing that came to mind.

"Get out! Will, you must get out of here this instant!"

"I refuse. You cannot leave—I will not allow it." A grin crossed his face. "You called me by my Christian name—I heard you so do not try to deny it."

She ignored him. The slip, using his name so carelessly, had tumbled from her lips. It was a minor infraction considering the wrongs they had all done her so recently.

"Get out, I said." He was not the only one who could be insistent. She lifted her chin, stared him in the eyes and repeated herself for a third time. "Get out—now!"

He chuckled, the sound sending a thrill up her spine despite her reluctance to be in any way affected by his presence.

"God, you are beautiful when you are angry. Although I do not intend to infuriate you more than I can help, Vivian. I promise, I shall try my best to keep from behaving so badly in the future."

She stared into his eyes, confused by not only his appearance but by the senseless conversation.

"What are you talking about? Have you lost your mind?" When he placed a hand over hers where it lay in her lap, she pushed his aside. He did not pull his hand away. It stayed on her skirt over her knee as if it had nowhere else to go.

Had he really taken leave of his senses?

Using a gentler tone of voice, hoping to encourage him to get out of the carriage, she asked, "Truly, are you all right? I mean, have you fallen on your head or hurt yourself in some way?"

A lazy thumb slid across the brown fabric she wore. The traveling dress was new but it was not fancy, and the rasp of his skin over the stiff material made a strange sound.

"I hurt us both, I am afraid. I should have spoken up yesterday when Oliver accused you of being something you are not—someone I know you could never be. I did not, and it is something I will regret forever." An exasperated huff punctuated the words. When he looked into her eyes, she saw how deeply he regretted what had happened.

It does not change things, she thought sadly. He may be sorry, but I still must leave.

"It is fine." It was the first forgiveness that had come without thought, and was genuine. "Do not condemn yourself over what has happened. What else could you think? Honestly, you do not know me well enough to see the real me."

"Wrong! You are wrong—as wrong as I was, almost. Why, I have seen the 'real you' from the very moment I first gazed at you. I have seen you, and been in love with you, almost from the minute you arrived. I could not believe my misfortune; you are just what I dreamed of my whole life and there you were, looking to make a match with my closest friend. I wanted to scream, but I did nothing. I watched you every day, and kept quiet when I should have spoken. I should have told you how I feel, even before I realized you and Oliver have no attachments. I will hate myself forever for not standing up for you yesterday—I was just so shocked by the rapid turn of events, and could hardly think, let alone speak!"

That was exactly how she had felt, so she understood completely.

"But I will not keep quiet now." He grabbed her hand and held it firmly between both of his. "I know my cottage is humble, but my situation is a secure one and I promise I will always look after you. I would like it if your family moved to Town so we could see them often. And, lest you think I have really and truly lost my mind, I want you to know I have been awake all night thinking of this very moment. I did not expect you would leave so early, or I would have been waiting by the front door to bar your departure."

She could not stand the suspense. Her head reeled, her heart thudded and her palms were suddenly clammy. Was it possible he felt the same way she did? Was it too much to ask, too high a dream?

"Will—stop it, you are confusing me with all you are saying. I do not understand—"

He took a deep breath, and the muscles flexed beneath his perspiration-soaked shirt. The sight made her heart skip a beat, but she did not have time to linger on his strong physique.

"I love you, Vivian. I have for weeks now. Will you forgive my behavior and consider my feelings for you?" He held her captive with his velvety brown gaze. "Will you marry me? Please, say yes."

Hurt feelings and misunderstandings aside, there was no denying her heart.

Vivian could hardly breathe, her chest was so tight. She nodded, and then smiled.

"I am also guilty of not speaking when I should, of not telling the truth when it is the only thing I can think of. I have loved you all this time. All this time, and yet I've been silent."

"Are you saying what I think you are?" He pulled her close, his mouth inches from hers. When she nodded, he claimed her lips with his in a kiss that was both tender and enthusiastic. Will pulled back. "Say it, Vivian. Say you will become my wife."

"I will…I will marry you and love every moment of being your wife."

"Thank God I have finally found my voice," he muttered hoarsely as he kissed her again.

And thank goodness I am here to hear it, my love…

A word about the author...

Sarita Leone loves adventure, whether it be in a distant continent or her own backyard. When she's not off exploring the world, she keeps busy writing, reading, and dancing beneath the stars. Always a fan of happy endings, she's fortunate to have a job which allows for so many of those!

She loves to hear from readers. Easiest way to connect? Check out her Facebook page, where all the latest news hits the screen.